I heard Sir Orfeo shout and I rolled over and looked for a hole to dive into and in that instant saw the wounded leech-thing flow down across the rock, disappear for a second behind a spur, come into view again just above Lord Desroy and the Lady Raire. Lord Desroy stood his ground, firing steadily into the leech-thing until the instant it struck full on him, covering him completely. It gathered itself together and lurched toward the Lady Raire, standing all alone in the trail, sixty feet behind where I was. As it moved, it left a trail of what was left of Lord Desroy.

The wounded leech was close to the Lady Raire now, and I saw then that she had no gun; Lord Desroy had been carrying it for her. She stood there, facing the thing, while Sir Orfeo poured the fire into it. At each shot, a chunk flew from its back, but it never slowed—and behind Sir Orfeo the other one was closing the gap.

GALACTIC
ODYSSEY

Look for all these Tor books by Keith Laumer

KEITH LAUMER

GALACTIC ODYSSEY

A TOM DOHERTY ASSOCIATES BOOK

GALACTIC ODYSSEY

Copyright © 1967 by Keith Laumer

All rights reserved, including the right to reproduce this book or portions thereof in any form.

A shorter version of this novel appeared serially in *If Magazine*, May-July, 1967 under the title *Spaceman*. Copyright © 1967, by Galaxy Publishing Corp.

First Tor printing: August 1983
Second printing: January 1987

A TOR Book

Published by Tom Doherty Associates, Inc.
49 West 24 Street
New York, N.Y. 10010

Cover art by Tom Kidd

ISBN: 0-812-54385-8
CAN. ED.: 0-812-54386-6

Printed in the United States of America

0 9 8 7 6 5 4 3 2 1

GALACTIC ODYSSEY

CHAPTER ONE

I remember hearing somewhere that freezing to death is an easy way to go; but the guy that said that never tried it. I'd found myself a little hollow where a falling-down stone wall met a dirt-bank, and hunkered down in it; but the wall wasn't high enough to keep the wind off or stop the sleet from hitting my neck like buckshot and running down cold under my collar. There were some moldy leaves drifted there, and I used the last of my lighter fluid trying to get a little blaze going, but that turned out like everything else I'd tried lately: a fizzle. One thing about it: My feet were so numb from the cold I couldn't feel the blisters from the eighteen miles I'd hiked since my last ride dumped me at a crossroads, just before dawn.

I had my collar turned up, for what good that might do, which wasn't much; the coat felt like wet newspaper. Both elbows were out of it, and two of the buttons were gone. Funny; three weeks ago it had been decent-looking enough to walk into a second-class restaurant in without attracting more than the usual quota of hostile stares. Three weeks: That's all it took to slide from a shaky toehold in the economic cycle all the way to the bottom. I'd heard of hitting the skids, but I never knew before just what it meant. Once you go over that invisible edge, it's downhill all the way.

It had been almost a year since I'd quit school, when Uncle Jason died. What money I had went for the cheapest funeral the little man with the sweet, sad smile could bear to talk about. After that, I'd held a couple of jobs that had wafted away like the morning mist as soon as the three months "tryout" was over and the question of regular wages came up. There'd been a few months of scrounging, then; mowing lawns, running errands, one-day stands as a carpenter's helper or assistant busboy while the regular man was off. I'd tried to keep up appearances, enough not to scare off any prospective employers, but the money barely stretched to cover food and what the sign said was a clean bed. Then one day I'd showed up looking just a little too thin, a little too hungry, the collar just a little too frayed.

And now I was here, with my stomach making whimpering sounds to remind me of all the meals it hadn't had lately, as far as ever from where I was headed—wherever that was. I didn't really have a destination. I just wanted to be where I wasn't.

And I couldn't stay here. The wall was worse than no protection at all, and the wind was blowing colder and wetter all the time. I crawled out and made it back up the slope to the road. There were no headlights in sight; it wouldn't have helped if there were. Nobody was going to stop in a sleetstorm in the middle of nowhere to give a lift to a hobo like me. I didn't have any little sign to hold up, stating that I was a hardship case, that comfortable middle-class conformity was my year of college who'd had a little hard luck lately; all I had were the clothes I stood in, a bad cough, and a deep conviction that if I didn't get out of the weather, fast, by morning I'd be one of those dead-of-exposure cases they're always finding in alleys back of cut-rate liquor stores.

I put my back to the wind and started off, hobbling on a couple of legs that ended somewhere below the knee. I didn't notice feeling tired anymore, or hungry; I was just a machine somebody had left running. All I could do was keep putting one foot in front of the other until I ran down.

I saw the light when I came up over a rise, just a weak little spark, glowing a long way off in the big dark beyond the trees. I turned and started off across the open field toward it.

Ten minutes later, I came up behind a big swaybacked barn with a new-looking silo beside it and a rambling two story house beyond. The light was shining from a ground-floor window. There was a pickup parked in the side yard near the barn, and a late-model Cadillac convertible, with the top down. Just looking at it made me ten degrees colder. I didn't have any idea of knocking on the door, introducing myself: "Billy Danger, sir. May I step inside and curl up in front of the fire?"— and being invited to belly up to a chicken dinner. But there was the barn; and where there were barns, there was hay; and where there was hay, a man could snuggle down and sleep, if not warm, at least not out in the freezing rain. It was worth a try.

The barn door looked easy enough: just warped boards hanging on big rusted-out hinges; but when I tried it, nothing budged. I looked closer, and saw that the hinges weren't rotted after all; they were just made to look that way. I picked at a flake of paint on the door; there was bright metal underneath. That was kind of strange, but all it meant to me then was that I wouldn't be crawling into that haystack after all.

The sleet was coming down thicker than ever now. I put my nose up and sniffed, caught a whiff of frying bacon and coffee that made my jaws ache. All of a sudden, my stomach remembered its complaint and tried to tie itself into a hard knot. I went back through tall weeds past some rusty iron that used to be farm machinery, and across a rutted drive toward the silo. I didn't know much about silos except that they were where you stored the corn, but at least it had walls and a roof. If I could get in there, I might find a dry spot to hide in. I reached a door set in the curved wall; it opened and I slid inside, into dim light and a flow of warm air.

Across the room, there was an inner door standing open, and I could see steps going up: glass steps on chrome-plated rails. The soft light and the warm air were coming from there. I went up, moving on instinct, like the first fish crawling out on land, reached the top and was in a room full of pipes and tubes and machinery and a smell like the inside of a TX set. Weary as I was, this didn't look like a place to curl up in.

I made it up another turn of the spiral stair, came out in a space where big shapes like cotton bales were stacked, with dark spaces between them. There was a smell like a fresh-tarred road here. I groped toward the deepest shadow I could find, and my hand touched something soft. In the faint light from the stairwell it looked like mink or sable, except that it was an electric-blue color. I didn't let that worry me. I crawled up on top of the stack and put my face down in the velvety fluff and let all the strings break at once.

In the dream, I was a burglar, holed up in somebody else's house, hiding in the closet, and in a minute they'd find me and haul me out and ride me into town in a police car to sit under the lights and answer questions about every unsolved chicken-stealing in the county in the past five years. The feet were coming up the stairs, coming closer. Somebody said something and a woman's voice answered in a foreign language. They went away and the dream faded. . . .

. . . And then the noise started.

It was a thin, high-pitched shrilling, like one of those whistles you call the dog with. It went right between my bones and pried at the joints. It got louder, and angrier, like bees boiling out of a hive, and I was awake now, and trying to get up; but a big hand came down and mashed me flat. I tried to get enough breath in to yell, but the air had turned to syrup. I just had time to remember the day back in Pineville when the Chevvy rolled off the rack at Uncle Jason's gas station and pinned a man under the back bumper. Then it all went red and I was someplace else, going over Niagara Falls in a big rubber balloon, wearing a cement life jacket, while thousands cheered.

When I woke up, I heard voices.

". . . talking rot now. It's nothing to do with me." This was a man's voice, speaking with an English accent. He sounded as if he were a little amused by something.

"I mark well t'was thee I charged with the integrity o' the vessel!" This one sounded big, and mad. He had a strange way of talking, but I could understand most of the words all right. Then a girl spoke, but in another language. She had a nice, clear, sweet voice. She sounded worried.

"No harm done, Desroy." The first man gave a soft laugh. "And it might be a spot of good luck, at that. Perhaps he'll make a replacement for Jongo."

"I don't omit thy ill-placed japery, Orfeo! Rid me this urchin, ere you vex me out of all humor!"

"A bit of a sticky wicket, that, old boy. He's still alive, you know. If I nurse him along—"

"How say you? What stuff is this! Art thou the parish comfort, to wax chirurgeonly o'er this whelp?"

"If he can be trained—"

"You o'ertax my patience, Orfeo! I'd make a chough of as deep chat!"

"He'll make a gun-boy, mark my words."

"Bah! You more invest the misadventure than a marketplace trinket chafferer! In any case, the imp's beyond recovery!"

Part of me wanted to just skip over this part of the dream and sink back down into the big, soft black that was waiting for me, but a little voice somewhere back behind my eyes was telling me to do something, fast, before bad things happened. I made a big effort and got one eyelid open. Everything looked red and hazy. The three of them were standing ten feet away, near the door. The one with the funny way of speaking was big, built solid as a linebacker, with slicked-back black hair and a little moustache. He wore a loose jacket covered with pockets; he looked like Clark Gable playing Frank Buck.

The other man was not much older than me; he had a rugged jawline, a short nose, curly reddish-brown hair, wide shoulders, slim hips in a form-fitting gray coverall. He was pretty enough to be a TV intern.

The girl . . . I had to stop and get the other eyelid up. No girl could be that pretty. She had jet black hair and smoky gray eyes big enough to go wading in; an oval face, mellow ivory-colored skin, features like one of those old statues. She was wearing a white coverall, and the form it fit was enough to break your heart.

I made a move to sit up and pain broke over me like a wave. It seemed to be coming mostly from my left arm. I took hold of the wrist with my other hand and got up on one elbow with no more effort than it takes to swing a safe in your teeth.

Nobody seemed to notice; when the whirly lights settled down, they were still standing there, still arguing.

". . . a spot of bother, Desroy, but it's worth a go."

"Methinks sloth instructs thee, naught else!" The big fellow turned and stamped off. The young fellow grinned at the girl.

"Just twisting the old boy's tail. Actually, he's right. You nip off and soothe him down a bit. I'll attend to this."

I slid over the edge of my nest and kind of fell to the floor. At the noise, they both whirled on me. I got hold of the floor and swung it around under me.

"I just came in to get out of the weather," I meant to say, but it came out as a sort of gargly sound. The man took a quick step toward me and over his shoulder said, "Pop off now, Milady." He had a hand on a thing clipped to his belt. I didn't need a set of technical specifications to tell me it was some kind of gun. The girl moved up quickly and put her hand on his arm.

"Orfeo—the poor creature suffers!" She spoke English with an accent that made it sound like music.

He moved her around behind him. "He might be dangerous. Now do be a good child and toddle off."

"I'm . . . not dangerous," I managed to get the words out. The smile was less successful. I felt sick. But I wasn't going to come unfed in front of *her*. I got my back against the pile of furs and tried to stand up straight.

"So you can talk," the man said. He was frowning at me. "Damn me if I know what to do with you." He seemed to be talking to himself.

"Just . . . let me rest a few minutes . . . and I'll be on my way . . ." I could hear my pulse thudding in my ears like bongo drums.

"Why did you come aboard?" The man snapped the question at me. "What did you think you'd find here?"

"I was cold," I said. "It was warm here—"

He snorted. "Letting yourself in for a devilish change of scene, weren't you?"

His first words were beginning to filter through. "What is this place?" I asked him.

"You're aboard Lord Desroy's yacht. He's not keen on contraband holed up in the aft lazaret—"

"A boat?" I felt I'd missed something somewhere. The last I remembered was a farmhouse, in the middle of nowhere. "You must be fooling me." I tried to show him a smile to let him know I got the joke. "I don't feel any waves."

"She's a converted ketch, stressed-field primaries, ion-pulse auxiliaries, fitted with full antiac and variable G gear, four years out of Zeridajh on a private expedition. Every square inch of her is allocated to items in specific support of her mission in life, which brings us back to you. What's your name?"

He asked that last in a businesslike tone.

"Billy Danger. I don't understand all that about a catch . . ."

"Just think of her as a small spaceship." He sounded impatient. "Now, Billy Danger, it's up to me to—"

"Spaceship? You mean like they shoot astronauts off in?"

Orfeo laughed. "Astronauts, eh? Couple of natives paddling about the shallows in a dugout canoe. No, Billy Danger, this is a deepspace yacht, capable of cruising for many centuries at multiple-light velocities. At the moment, she's on course for a world very distant from your native Earth."

"Wait a minute," I said; I wanted everything to slow down for just a second while I got caught up with it. "I don't want to go to any star. I just want out of here." I tried to step and had to lean against the bale beside me. "Just let me off, and I'll disappear so quick you'll think you dreamed me—"

"I'm afraid that's not practical." Orfeo cut me off short. "Now you're here, the question is what to do with you. As you doubtless heard, Lord Desroy's in favor of putting you out the lock. As for myself, I have hopes of making use of you. Know anything about weapons? Hunted much?"

"Just let me off," I said. "Anywhere at all. I'll walk home."

"You must answer my questions promptly, Billy Danger! What becomes of you depends on how well you answer them."

"I never hunted," I said. My breath was short, as if I'd run a long way.

"That's all right. Nothing to unlearn. How old are you?"

"Nineteen, next April."

"Amazing. You look younger. Are you quick to learn, Billy Danger?"

"It's kidnaping," I said. "You can't just kidnap a man. There's laws—"

"Mind your tongue, Billy Danger! I'll tolerate no insolence, you'd best understand that at the outset! As for law, Lord Desroy makes the law here. This is his vessel; with the exception of the Lady Raire and myself, he owns every atom aboard her, including stowaways."

A sudden thought occurred to me, like an icepick through the heart. "You're not . . . Earthmen, are you?"

"Happily, no."

"But you look human; you speak English."

"Of course we're human; much older stock than your own unfortunate branch. We've spent a year on your drab little world, going after walrus, elephant, that sort of thing. Now, that's enough chatter, Billy Danger. Do you think you can learn to be a proper gun-bearer?"

"How long—before we go back?"

"To Earth? Never, I trust. Now, see here! Don't fret about matters out of your control! Your job is to keep me happy with you. If you can do that, you'll stay alive and well. If not . . ." He let the rest hang. "But then, I'm sure you'll try your best, eh, Billy Danger?"

It was crazy, but the way he said it, I believed every word of it. The thing I had to do right now was stay alive. Then, later, I could worry about getting home.

"Sure," I said. "I'll try."

"Right. That's settled, then." Orfeo looked relieved, as if he'd just found an excuse to put off a mean chore. "You were lucky, you know. You took eight gravities, unprotected. A wonder you didn't break a few bones."

I was still holding my left arm by the wrist; I eased it around front, and felt the sharp point poking out through my sleeve.

"Who said I didn't?" I asked him, and felt myself folding like a windblown newspaper.

CHAPTER TWO

I woke up feeling different. At first, I couldn't quite dope out what it was; then I got it: I was clean, fresh-shaved, sweet-smelling, tucked in between sheets as crisp as new dollar bills. And I felt good; I tingled all over, as if I'd just had a needle shower and a rubdown.

The room I was in was a little low-ceilinged cubbyhole with nothing much in it but the pallet I was lying on. I remembered the arm then, and pulled back a loose yellow sleeve somebody had put on me. Outside of a little swelling and a bright pink scar under a clear plastic patch, it was as good as new.

Something clicked and a little door in the wall slid back. The man named Orfeo stuck his head in.

"Good; you're awake. About time. I'm about to fieldstrip the Z-guns. You'll watch."

I got up and discovered that my knees didn't wobble anymore. I felt strong enough to run up a wall. And hungry. Just thinking about ham and eggs made my jaws ache. Orfeo tossed me a set of yellow coveralls from a closet back of a sliding panel.

"Try these; I cut them down from Jongo's old cape."

I pulled them on. The cloth was tough and light and smooth as glove silk.

"How are you feeling?" Orfeo was looking me up and down.

"Fine," I said. "How long did I sleep?"

"Ninety-six hours. I doped you up a bit."

I ran a finger over my new scar. "I don't understand about the arm. I remember it as being broken; broken bad—"

"A hunter has to know a little field medicine," he said. "While I was about it, I gave you a good worming and balanced up your body chemistry." He shook his head. "Bloody wonder you could walk, the rot that boiled out of you. Bloody microbe culture. How's your vision?"

I blinked at the wall. If there'd been a fly there, I could have counted his whiskers. "Good," I said. "Better than it's ever been."

"Well, you're no good to me sick," as if he had to apologize.

"Thanks," I said. "For the arm, and the bath and the pretty yellow pajamas, too."

"Don't thank me. The Lady Raire took care of that part."

"You mean . . . the girl?"

"She's the Lady Raire, Jongo! And I'm Sir Orfeo. As for the wash-up and the kit, someone had to do it. You stank to high heaven. Now come along. We've a great deal to cover if you're to be of any use to me on the hunt."

The armory was a small room lined with racks full of guns that weren't like any guns I'd ever seen before. There were handguns, rifles, rocket-throwers, some with short barrels some with just a bundle of glass rods, some with fancy telescopic sights, one that looked like a flare pistol with a red glass thermometer on the side; and there were a few big elephant guns of Earth manufacture. The whole room glittered like Tiffany's front window. I ran a finger along a stock made of polished purple wood, with fittings that looked like solid gold. "It looks like Mister Desroy goes first class."

"Keep your hands off the weapons until you know how to service them." Sir Orfeo poked buttons and a table tilted up out of the floor and a section of ceiling over it glared up brighter than before. He flipped a switch and the lock-bar on a rack snapped up, and he lifted out a heavy-looking, black-stocked item with a drum magazine and three triggers and a flared shoulder plate, chrome-plated.

"This is a Z-gun," he said. "It's a handy all-round piece, packs 0.8 megaton/seconds of firepower, weight four pounds three ounces." He snapped a switch on the side back and forth a couple of times and handed the gun across to me.

"What's a megaton/second?" I asked him.

"Enough power to vaporize the yacht if it were released at one burst. At full gain the Z-gun will punch a three-millimeter hole through an inch of flint steel at a range of five miles with a five millisecond burst." He went on to tell me a lot more about Z-guns, crater-rifles, infinite repeaters, filament pistols.

At the end of it I didn't know much more about the weapons Lord Desroy would be using on his hunt, but I was feeling sorry for whatever it was he was after.

Sir Orfeo took me back to the little room I'd waked up in, showed me how to work a gadget that delivered a little can of pink oatmeal, steaming hot. I sniffed it; it smelled like seaweed. I tasted it. It was flat and insipid, like papier-mâché.

"Sir Orfeo, I hate to complain about a free gift," I said. "But are you sure this was meant for a man to eat?"

"Jongo wasn't a man."

I kind of goggled at him. "What was he?"

"A Lithian. Very good boy, Jongo. With me for a long time." He glanced around the room. "Damned if it doesn't give me a touch of some-thing-or-other to see you in his kennel."

"Kennel?"

"Nest, pitch, call it cabin if you like." Sir Orfeo beetled a fine eyebrow at me. "Don't be putting on airs, Billy Danger. I've no patience with it."

He left me there to dine in solitude. After-ward, he gave me a tour of the ship. He was showing me a fancy leather-and-inlay lounge when Lord Desroy came in.

"Ah, there you are, Desroy," Orfeo said in a breezy way. "Just occurred to me you might like to have Jongo—ah, Billy Danger, that is—do a bit of a dust-up here in the lounge—"

"How now? Hast lost thy wits, Orfeo? Hie the mooncalf hence i' the instant!"

"Steady on, Desroy. Just thought I'd ask—"

"I've a whim to chide the varlet for his im-pertinence!" the big boss barked and took a step toward me. Orfeo pushed me behind him.

"Don't blame the boy. My doing, you know," he said in a nice cool tone.

"Thy role of advocate for this scurvy patch would want credit, an' I stood not witness on't!"

We went on down the stairs. Instead of look-ing mad, Sir Orfeo was smiling and humming between his teeth. He dropped the smile when he saw me looking at him.

"I advise you to stay out of Lord Desroy's way, Jongo. For now, he's willing to humor me along; I have a carefully nurtured reputation for temperament, you see. If I get upset, the game might turn out to be scarce. But if you ruffle his feathers by being underfoot, he might act hastily."

"He has a strange way of talking," I said. "What kind of accent is that?"

"Eh? Oh, it's a somewhat archaic dialect of English. Been some three hundred years since his lordship last visited Earth. Now, that's enough gossip, Jongo—"

"It's Billy Dan—"

"I'll call you Jongo. Shorter. Now let's get along to Hold F and you can earn your keep by polishing a spot of brightwork in Environmental."

The polishing turned out to be a job of scraping slimy deposits off the valves and piping. Sir Orfeo left me to it while he went back up and joined in whatever they were doing on the other side of the forbidden door.

One day Sir Orfeo showed me a star chart and pointed out the relative locations of Earth, Gar 28, the world we were headed for at the moment, and Zeridajh, far in toward the big gob of stars at the center of the Galaxy.

"We'll never get there," I said. "I read somewhere it takes light a hundred thousand years to cross the Galaxy; Gar 28 must be about ten light-years away; and Zeridajh is thousands!"

He laughed. "The limiting velocity of light is a myth, Jongo," he said. "Like the edge of the world your early sailors were afraid they'd fall over—or the sound barrier you used to worry about. This vessel could reach Zeridajh in eighteen months, if she stretched her legs."

I wanted to ask him why Lord Desroy picked such a distant part of the sky to go hunting in, but I'd learned not to be nosy. Whatever the reasons were, they were somebody's secret.

After my first few weeks away from all time indicators, I began to develop my own internal time-sense, independent of the three-hour cycles that were the Galactic shipboard standard. I could sense when an hour had passed, and looking back, I knew, without knowing how I knew, just about how long I'd been away from Earth. I might have been wrong —there was no way to check—but the sense was very definite, and always consistent.

I had been aboard just under six weeks when Sir Orfeo took me to the personal equipment room one day and fitted me out with thermal boots, leggings, gloves, a fancy pair of binocular sunglasses, breathing apparatus,

a backpack, and a temperature suit. He spent
an hour fussing over me, getting everything
fitted just right. Then he told me to go and tie
down in my digs. I did, and for the next hour
the yacht shook and shrilled and thumped.
When the noise stopped, Sir Orfeo came along
and yelled to me to get into my kit and come
down to F Hold. When I got there, walking
pretty heavy with all the gear I was carrying
or had strapped to my back, he was there,
checking items off a list.

"A little more juldee next time, Jongo," he
snapped at me. "Come along now; I'll want
your help in getting the ground-car out ship-
shape."

It was a powerful-looking vehicle, wide,
squatty, with tracks like a small tank, a
plastic bubble dome over the top. There was a
roomy compartment up front full of leather
and inlaid wood and bright work, and a smaller space behind, with two hard seats. Lord
Desroy showed up in his Frank Buck bush
jacket and jodhpurs and a wide-brimmed hat;
the Lady Raire wore her white coverall. Sir
Orfeo was dressed in his usual tailored gray
with a filament pistol strapped to his hip and
a canteen and bush knife on the other side. We
all wore temperature suits, which were like
long-handled underwear, under the coveralls.
"Keep your helmet closed, Jongo," Sir Orfeo
told me. "Toxic atmosphere, you know."

He pushed a button and a door opened up in
the side of the hold, and I was looking out at a

plain of bluish grass. A wave of heat rolled in and the thermostat in my suit clicked, and right away it turned cool against my skin. Sir Orfeo started up and the car lifted a couple of inches from the floor, swung around, and slid out under the open sky of a new world.

For the next hours I perched on my seat with my mouth open, taking in the sights: the high, blue-black sky, strange trees like over-grown parsley sprigs, the leathery grass that stretched to a horizon that was too far away—and the animals. The things we were after were big crab-armored monstrosities, pale purple and white, with mouths full of needle-pointed teeth and horns all over their faces. Lord Desroy shot two of them, stopping the car and going forward on foot. I guess it took courage, but I didn't see the point in it. Each time, he and Sir Orfeo made a big thing of hacking off one of the horns and taking a lot of pictures and congratulating each other. The Lady Raire just watched from the car. She didn't seem to smile much.

We loaded up and went on to another world then, and Milord shot a thing as big as a diesel locomotive. Sir Orfeo never talked about himself or the other members of the party, or the world they came from, but he explained the details of the hunt to me, gave me pointers on tracking and approaching, told me which gun to use for different kinds of quarry. Not much of it stuck. After the fourth or fifth hunt, it all got a little stale.

"This next world is called Gar 28," Sir
Orfeo woke me up to tell me after a long
stretch in space. "Doesn't look like much; dry,
you know; but there'll be keen hunting. I
found this one myself, running through tapes
made by a survey team a few hundred years
ago. The fellows we'll be going after they
called dire-beast. You'll understand why
when you see the beggars."

He was right about Gar 28. We started out
across a rugged desert of dry-baked pink and
tan and yellow clay, fissured and cracked by
the sun, with points of purplish rock pushing
up here and there, a line of jagged peaks for a
horizon. It didn't look like game country to
me, but then I wasn't the hunter.

The sun was high in the sky, too bright to
look at, a little smaller than the one I was
used to. It was cool and comfortable inside
the car; it hummed along a couple of feet
above the ground, laying a dust trail behind it
from the air blast it was riding on. The tracks
were for hills that were too steep for the air
cushion to climb.

About a mile from the yacht, I looked back;
it was just a tiny glint, like a lost needle,
among all that desolation.

Up front, on the other side of the glass
panel, Lord Desroy and Sir Orfeo and the
Lady Raire chatted away in their odd language, and every now and then said something
in that strange brand of English they spoke. I
could hear them through a speaker hookup in

the back of the car. If I'd had something to say, I don't know whether they could have heard it or not.

After two hours' run, we pulled up at the top of a high escarpment. Sir Orfeo opened the hatch, and we all got out. I remembered Sir Orfeo had told me always to stay close with his gun when we were out of the car so I got out one of the crater-rifles and came up behind them in time to see Sir Orfeo point.

"There—by the double peak at the far end of the faultline!" He snapped his goggles up and whirled to start back and almost slammed into me. A very thin slice of an instant later I was lying on my back with my head swimming, looking into the operating end of his filament pistol.

"Never come up behind me with a weapon in your hand!"

I got up, with my head still whanging from the blow he'd hit me, and followed them to the car, and we went tearing back down the slope the way we'd come.

It was a fast fifteen-minute run out across the flats toward where Sir Orfeo had seen whatever it was he saw. I had my binocular goggles on and was looking hard, but all I saw was the dusty plain and the sharp rock spires, growing taller as we rushed toward them. Then Sir Orfeo swung the car to the left in a wide curve and pulled to a stop behind a low ridge.

"Everybody out!" he snapped, and popped

the hatch up and was over the side.

"Don't sit there and brood, Jongo!" He was grinning, excited and happy now. "My crater-rifle; Z-guns for his lordship and Lady Raire!"

I handed the weapons down to him, stock-first, the way he'd told me.

"You'll carry the extra crater and a fila-ment pistol," he said, and moved back up front to go into conference with the others. I strapped on the Z-gun and grabbed the rifle and hopped down just as Sir Orfeo and Lord Desroy started off. The Lady Raire followed about ten feet back, and I took up my post off-side to the right about five yards. My job was to keep that relative position to Sir Orfeo, no matter what, until he yelled "Close!" Then I was to move in quick. That was about all I knew about a hunt. That, and don't come up behind Sir Orfeo with a gun.

The sun still seemed to be about where it had been when we started out. There was a little wind blowing from behind, keeping a light cloud of dust rolling along ahead. It seemed to me I'd heard somewhere that you were supposed to sneak up on game from up-wind, but that wasn't for me to worry about. All I had to do was maintain my interval. We came to a slight rise of ground. The wind was picking up, driving a thick curtain of dust ahead. For a few seconds I couldn't see any-thing but that yellow fog swirling all around. I stopped and heard a sound, a deep *thoom! thoom! thoom!*

"Close! Damn your eyes, Jongo, close!" Sir Orfeo shouted. I ran toward the sound of his voice, tripped over a rock, and went flat. I could hear Lord Desroy shouting something and the *thoom-thoom*, louder than before. I scrambled up and ran on forward, and as suddenly as it had blown up, the gale died and the dust rolled away from us. Sir Orfeo was twenty feet off to my left, with Lord Desroy beside him. I changed direction and started toward them, and saw Sir Orfeo make a motion, and Lord Desroy brought his rifle up and I looked where he was aiming and out of the dust cloud a thing came galloping that was right out of a nightmare. It was big— twenty, thirty feet high, running on two legs that seemed to have too many knees. The feet were huge snowshoelike pads, and they rose and fell like something in a slow-motion movie, driving dust from under them in big spurts, and at each stride the ground shook. A second one came charging out of the dust cloud, and it was bigger than the first one. Their hides were a glistening greenish brown, except where they were coated with dust, and there was a sort of cape of ragged skin flapping from the narrow shoulders of one as he ran, and I thought he must be shedding. Thick necks rose from the shoulders, with wide flat heads that were all mouth, like the bucket of a drag-line. And then a third, smaller edition came scampering after the big fellows.

All this happened in maybe a second or two.

I had skidded to a halt and was standing there, in a half crouch, literally paralyzed. I couldn't have moved if an express train had been coming straight at me. And these were worse than express trains.

They were about a hundred and fifty yards away when Lord Desroy fired. I heard the Z-gun make a sharp whickering noise and an electric-blue light flashed up and lit the rocks like lightning, and the lead monster broke stride and veered off to the left, running irregularly now. He leaned, losing his balance, but still driving on, his neck whipped back and up and the head flailed offside as he went down, hit, bounced half upright, his legs still pumping, then went into a tumble of flailing legs and neck and the dust closed over him and only then I heard the shuddering boom he made hitting the ground.

And the second one was still coming, closer now than number one had been when he was hit, and the little fellow—a baby, only fifteen feet high—sprinted up alongside him, tilted his head sideways, and snapped at his big brother's side. I saw a flash of white as the hide and muscle tore; then the little one was skidding to a halt on his haunches, his big jaws working hard over the bite he'd gotten, while the one that had supplied the snack came on, looming up as high as a two-story house, black blood streaming down his flank, coming straight at Lord Desroy. I saw the Lady Raire then, just beyond him, right in the path of the charge; and still I couldn't move. Lord Desroy had his gun up again and it flickered and flashed and made its slapping noise and the biped's head, that it had been carrying high on its long neck, drooped and the neck went slack and the head came down and hit the ground and the big haunches, with the big feet still kicking, went up and over high in the air in a somersault and slammed the ground with a smash like two semi's colliding, and flipped up and went over again with one leg swinging out at a crazy angle and the other still pumping, and then it was looping the loop on the ground, kicking up a dust cloud that hid everything beyond it.

"Watch for baby!" Sir Orfeo yelled, and I could barely hear his voice through the thudding and pounding. Then the little one stalked out of the dust, tossing his head to help him swallow down what he had in his mouth. Sir Orfeo brought his gun up and the cub was coming straight at me, and the gun tracked him and went off with a flat *crackkk!* that kicked a pit the size of a washtub in the rock beside him and the young one changed direction and trotted off and Sir Orfeo let him go.

The dust was blowing away now, except for what number two was still kicking up with one foot that was twitching, still trying to run. Lord Desroy and Sir Orfeo went over to it, and the hunter used his pistol to put it out of its misery. It went slack and a gush of fluid sluiced out of its mouth and it was quiet.

"In sooth, the beast raised a din to make the ground quake," Lord Desroy called in a light-hearted tone. He walked around the creature, and Sir Orfeo went over to the other one, and about then I got my joints unlocked and trotted after him. Sir Orfeo looked up as I came up and gave me a grin.

"I think perhaps you'll make a gun-boy yet, Jongo," he said. "You were a bit slow coming up, but you held steady as a rock during the charge."

And for some reason I felt kind of ashamed of myself, knowing how it had really been.

Lord Desroy spent a quarter of an hour taking movies of the dead animals; then we made the hike back to the car.

"We were lucky, Desroy," Sir Orfeo told him as we settled into our seats. "Takes a bit of doing to knock over a fine brace on the first stalk! I suggest we go back to the yacht now and call it a day—"

"What foolery's this?" Lord Desroy boomed out. "Wi' a foison o' quarry to hand, ye'd skulk back to thy comforts wi'out further sweat or endeavor?"

"No use pushing our luck—"

"Prithee, spare! Ye spoke but now of bull-devil, lurking in the crags yonder—"

"Plenty of time to go after them later."
Orfeo was still smiling, but there was an edge
to his voice. He didn't like to have anyone
argue with him about a hunt.

"A pox on't" Lord Desroy slammed his fist
down on the arm of his chair. "Dost dream I'd
loiter in my chambers with game abounding?
Drive on, I say, or I'll take the tiller self!"

Sir Orfeo slapped the drive lever in and the
engines started up with a howl.

"I was thinking of the Lady Raire," he said.
"If you're that dead-set on running us all ragged, very well! Though what the infernal rush
is, I'm sure I don't know!"

As usual, the Lady Raire sat by quietly,
looking cool and calm and too beautiful to be
real. Lord Desroy got out a silver flask and
poured out yellow wine for her and himself,
then lolled back in his chair and gazed out at
the landscape rushing past.

An hour brought us to the foothills of the
range that had been visible from the yacht.
The going was rougher here; we switched over
to tracks for the climb. Lord Orfeo had quit
humming to himself and was beginning to
frown, as if maybe he was thinking about how
nice it would be to be back in his apartment
aboard the yacht, having a bath and a nice dinner, instead of being in for another four
hours, minimum, in the car.

We came out on a high plateau, and Sir
Orfeo pulled the car in under a steep escarpment and opened up and climbed down with-

out a word to anybody. I had his crater-rifle
ready for him; I took the other guns and got
out and Lord Desroy looked around and said
something I didn't catch.

"They're here, right enough," Sir Orfeo answered him, sounding mad. He walked off and
Lord Desroy and the girl trailed. I had to
scramble up on rough ground to get to my
proper position off to Sir Orfeo's right. He
was headed into a narrow cut that curved up
and away in deep shadow. The sun still seemed to be in the same spot, directly overhead.
My suit kept me comfortable enough, but the
heat reflecting back from the stone scalded
my face.

Sir Orfeo noticed me working my way along
up above him and snarled something about
where the devil did I think I was going; I
didn't try to answer that. I'd gotten myself
onto a ledge that ran along twenty feet above
the trail, with no way down. I stayed abreast
of Sir Orfeo and looked for my chance to re-
join the party.

We kept going this way, nobody talking, the
happy look long gone from Lord Desroy's face
now, the Lady Raire walking just to his left,
Sir Orfeo out in front twenty paces. The trail
did a sharp jog to the left, and I had to scramble to catch up; as I did, I saw something move
on the rocks up ahead.

Being above the rest of them, I had a view
past the next outcropping that hung out over

the trail; the movement I saw was just a flicker of something in the shadows, spread out flat on the rock like a giant leech. I felt my heart take a jump and jam itself up in my throat and I tried to yell and choked and tried again:

"Sir Orfeo! Up ahead! On the right!"

He stopped dead, swung his gun around and up, at the same time motioned to the others to halt. Lord Desroy checked for just a moment; then he stared on up toward Sir Orfeo. The animal—creature—thing—whatever it was—moved again. Now I could see what looked like an eye near the front, surrounded by a fringe of stiff reddish hairs. I got just the one quick look before I heard the whisper of a Z-gun from below, and the thing jerked back violently and disappeared into black shadow. Down below, Lord Desroy was lowering his gun.

"Well, that tears it!" Sir Orfeo said in a too loud voice. "Nice bit of shooting, Desroy! You failed to keep to your position, fired without any permission, and then succeeded in wounding the beggar! Anything else you'd care to try before we go into that cranny after him?"

"Methinks you skirt insolence, Orfeo," Lord Desroy started.

"Not intentionally, as I'm damned!" Orfeo's face was red; I could see the flush from where I was perched, twenty feet above him. "I'll re-

mind you *I'm* master of the hunt, *I'm* responsible for the safety of the party—"

"I'm out of patience wi' cautious counsel!"
Lord Desroy roared. "Shall I be merely cheated o' my sport whilst I attend your swoons?"

Sir Orfeo started to answer that, then
caught himself and laughed.

" 'Pon my word, you have a way about you,
Milord! Now, I suggest we give over this tom-
foolery and give a thought to how we're going
to get him out of there!" He turned and
squinted up toward the place where the thing
had disappeared.

"I warrant ye make mockery of me," Lord
Desroy growled. He jerked his head in my
direction. "Despatch yon natural to draw
forth the beast!" Sir Orfeo looked up, too,
then back at his boss.

"The boy's new, untrained," he said. "That's
a risky bit of business—"

"D'ye aver thy gun-boy lacks spirit, then?"

Sir Orfeo gave me a sharp look. "By no
means," he said. "He's steady enough. Jongo!" His voice changed tone. "Press on a few
yards, see if you can rout the blighter out."

I didn't move. I just squatted where I was
and stared down at him. The next instant,
something smashed against the wall beside
my head and knocked me sprawling. I came
up spitting dust, with my head ringing, and
Lord Desroy's second shot crashed close
enough to drive stone chips into my cheek.

"Sir Orfeo!" I got the yell out. "He's shooting at *me*!"

I heard Sir Orfeo shout and I rolled over and looked for a hole to dive into and in that instant saw the wounded leech-thing flow down across the rock, disappear for a second behind a spur, come into view again just above the trail, about thirty feet above Lord Desroy, between him and the Lady Raire. It must have made some sound I couldn't hear; before I could shout, Lord Desroy whirled and brought his gun up and it crackled and vivid shadows winked on the rocks and the animal leaped out and down, broad as a blanket, leathery dark, right into the gun. Lord Desroy stood his ground, firing steadily into the leech-thing until the instant it struck full on him, covering him completely. It gathered itself together and lurched toward the Lady Raire, standing all alone in the trail, sixty feet behind where I was. As it moved, it left a trail of what was left of Lord Desroy.

Sir Orfeo had fired once, while the thing was in the air. He ran toward it, stopped and took aim and fired again. I saw a movement off to the right, up the trail, and a second leech-thing was there, coming up fast behind Sir Orfeo, big as a hippopotamus, wide and flat and with its one eye gleaming green.

I yelled. He didn't look up, just stood where he was, his back to the leech, firing, and firing again. The wounded leech was close to the

Lady Raire now, and I saw then that she had
no gun, and I remembered that Lord Desroy
had taken it and had been carrying it for her.
She stood there, facing the thing, while Sir
Orfeo poured the fire into it. At each shot, a
chunk flew from its back, but it never
slowed—and behind Sir Orfeo the other one
was closing the gap. Sir Orfeo could have
turned his fire on it and saved himself; but he
never budged. I realized I was yelling at the
top of my lungs, and then I remembered I had
a gun, too, slung across my back to free my
hands for climbing. I grabbed for it, wasted a
second or more fumbling with it, got it
around and to my shoulder and aimed and
couldn't find the firing stud and had to lower
it and look and brought it up again and centered it on the thing only yards from Sir Orfeo's
exposed back and squeezed—

The recoil almost knocked me off my feet,
not that it was bad, but I wasn't expecting it. I
got back on target and fired again, and again;
and it kept coming. Six feet from Sir Orfeo the
thing reared up, tall as a grizzly, and I got a
glimpse of a yellow underside covered with
shredding hooks, and I fired into it and then it
was dropping down on Sir Orfeo and at the
last possible second he moved, but not far
enough, and the thing struck him and knocked
him rolling, and then he and it lay still. I traversed the gun across to the other beast and
saw that it was down, ten feet from Milady
Raire, bucking and writhing, coiling back on

itself. It flopped up against the side wall and rolled back down, half on its back, and lay still and the echoes of its struggle went racketing away up the ravine. I heard Sir Orfeo make a moaning sound where he lay all bloody and the Lady Raire looked up and her eyes met mine and we looked at each other across the terrible silence.

CHAPTER THREE

Sir Orfeo was still alive, with all the flesh torn off the back of his thighs and the glistening white bone showing.

He caught at my arm when I bent over him.

"Jongo—your job now—the Lady Raire . . ."

I was shaking and tears were running down my face. I tried not to look at his horrible wounds.

"Buck up, man," Sir Orfeo's voice was a groan of agony. "I'm depending on you . . . keep her safe . . . your responsibility, now. . . ."

"Yes," I said. "I'll take care of her, Sir Orfeo."

"Good . . . now . . . water. Fetch water . . . from the car. . . ."

I ran off to follow his orders. When I came

back the Lady Raire met me, looking pale and with dust sticking to the perspiration on her forehead. She told me that he'd sent her to investigate a sound and then dragged himself to where his filament pistol had fallen and blown his head off.

I used a crater-rifle to blast shallow pockets under the overhanging rock beside the trail; she helped me drag the bodies to them. Then we went back down to the car. We carried our guns at the ready, but nothing moved in all that jumble of broken rock. Sir Orfeo had been lucky about finding game, all right.

The Lady Raire got into the driver's seat and headed back down the way we'd come. When we reached level ground, she stopped and looked around as if she didn't know which way to go. I tapped on the glass and her head jerked around. I think she had forgotten I was there. Poor Lady Raire, so all-alone.

"That direction, Milady," I said, and pointed toward where the yacht was, out of sight over the horizon.

She followed my directions; three hours later we came up over a low ridge and there was the yacht, glittering far away across the desert. Another forty-five minutes and we pulled up in front of the big cargo door.

She jumped down and went to it and twinkled her fingers on a polished metal disc set in the hull beside it. Nothing happened. She went around to the smaller personnel door and the same thing happened. Then she looked at me. Having her look at me was an event even then.

"We cannot enter," she said in a whisper. "I mind well 'twas Sir Orfeo's custom to reset the entry code 'ere each planetfall lest the yacht be rifled by aborigines."

"There's got to be a way," I said. I went up and hammered on the panel and on the control disc and walked all the way around the yacht and back to the door that I had sneaked in by, that first night, and tried again, but with no luck. A terrible, hollow feeling was growing inside me.

"I can shoot a hole in it, maybe," I said. My voice sounded weak in the big silence. I unslung the crater-rifle and asked her to step back, and then took aim from ten feet and fired. The blast knocked me down, but the metal wasn't even scorched.

I got to my feet and brushed dust off my shins, feeling the full impact of the situation sinking in like the sun that was beating down on my back. The Lady Raire looked at me, not seeing me.

"We must . . . take stock of what supplies may be in the car," she said after a long pause. "Then can'st thou make for thyself a pallet here in the shadow of the boat."

"You mean—we're just going to sit here?"

"If any rescue comes, we must be close by the yacht, else they'll not spy us in this endless waste."

I took a deep breath and swallowed hard. "Milady, we can't stay here."

"Indeed? Why can we not?" She stood there, a slim, aristocratic little girl, giving me a level look from those cool gray eyes.

"I don't know much about the odds against anybody finding us, but we've got a long wait, at best. The supplies in the car won't last long. And the heat will wear us down. We have to try to find a better spot, now, while we're still strong." I tried to sound confident, as if I knew what I was doing. But my voice shook. I was scared; scared sick. But I knew I was right about moving on.

" 'Tis a better thing to perish here than to live on in the wilderness, without hope."

"We're not dead yet, Milady. But we will be if we don't do something about it, now."

"I'll tarry here," she said. "Flee if thou wilt, Jongo."

"Sir Orfeo told me to take care of you, Milady. I'm going to do my best to follow his order."

She looked at me coolly. "Wouldst force me, then?"

"I'm afraid so, Milady."

She walked to the car stiffly; I got into my usual seat in back and she started up and we headed out across the desert.

We drove until the sun set and a huge, pock-marked moon rose, looking a lot like the old one back home, except that it was almost close enough to touch. We slept then, and went on, still in the dark. Day came again, and I asked the Lady Raire to show me how to drive so I could relieve her at the wheel. After that, we drove shift on, shift off, holding the course steady to the northwest. On what I estimated was the third day, Earth-style, we reached a belt of scrub-land. Half an hour later the engine made a gargly sound and died, and wouldn't go again.

I went forward on foot to a rise and looked over the landscape. The scrub-dotted waste went on, as far as I could see. When I got back to the car, the Lady Raire was standing beside it with a filament pistol in her hand.

"Now indeed is our strait hopeless," she held the gun out to me. "Do thy final duty to me, Jongo." Her voice was a breathless whisper.

I took the gun; then I whirled and threw it as far as I could. When I faced her, my hands were shaking.

"Don't ever say anything like that again!" I said. "Not ever!"

"Would you then have me linger on, to wither in this heat, shrivel under the sun—"

I grabbed her arm. It was cool, as smooth as satin. "I'm going to take care of you, Milady," I said. "I'll get you home again safe, you'll see!"

She shook her head. "I have no home, Jongo; my loyal friends are dead—"

"I'm still alive. And my name's not Jongo. It's Billy Danger. I'm human, too. I'll be your friend."

She looked straight at me. It was the first time she ever really looked at me. I looked back, straight into her eyes. Then she smiled.

"Thou art valiant, Billy Danger," she said. "How can I then shrink from duty? Lead on, and I'll follow while my strength lasts."

The car was stocked with food concentrates, plus a freezer full of delicacies that would have to be eaten first, before they spoiled. The problem was water. The tanks held about thirty gallons, but with the distiller out of action, there'd be no refilling them. There were the weapons and plenty of ammunition, first-aid supplies, some spare communicators, goggles, boots. It wasn't much to set up housekeeping on.

For the next week, I quartered the landscape over a radius of about five miles, looking for a spring or water hole, with no luck.

By that time, the fresh food was gone—eaten or spoiled, and the water was down to two ten-gallon jugs full.

"We'll have to try a longer hike," I told the Lady Raire. "There may be an oasis just one ridge farther than I've gone."

"As you wish, Billy Danger," she said, and gave me that smile, like sunrise after a long night.

We packed up the food and water and a few extras. I slung a Z-gun over my shoulder, and started off at twilight, after the worst of the day's heat.

It was monotonous country, just hilly enough to give us a long pull up to one low crest after another and an ankle-turning slog down the far side. I steered due west, not because the prospects looked any better in that direction, but just because it was easier to steer straight toward the setting sun.

We did about twenty miles before dark, another forty in two marches before the sun rose. I worried about the Lady Raire, but there was nothing I could do that I wasn't already doing. We slogged on toward the next ridge, hoping for a miracle on the other side. And always the next side looked the same.

We rested in the heat of the long day, then marched on, into the glare of the sun. And about an hour before sunset, we saw the cat.

He was standing on a rock on the crest of a rise, whipping his tail from side to side in a slow, graceful motion. He made a graceful leap to a lower rock and was just a dark sha- dow moving against the slope ahead. I unlimb- ered my rifle and watched him close. At thirty feet, he paused and sat down on his haunches and wrinkled his face and began licking his chest. He finished and stuck out a long tongue and yawned, and then rose and went loping off into the dusk, the way he'd come.

All the while, we stood there and watched him, not saying a word. As soon as he was gone, I went to where he'd been sitting. His paw-prints were plain in the powdery dust. I started believing in him, then. I might see imaginary cats, but never imaginary cat tracks. We set off following them as fast as we could in the failing light.

The water hole was in a hollow in the rock, hidden behind a wall of black-green foliage growing on the brink of a ravine. The Lady Raire stopped to gaze at it, but I stumbled down the slope and fell full-length in the water and drank in big gulps and luckily choked and had a coughing fit before I could drink myself to death.

There was a steep jumble of rock rising behind the pool, with the dark mouths of caves showing. I picked my way around the pond in the near-dark with my gun ready in my hand. There was a smell of cat in the air. I was grateful to tabby for leading me to water, but I didn't want him jumping on our backs now that it looked like we might live another few days.

The caves weren't much, just holes about ten feet deep, not quite high enough to stand up in, with enough dirt drifted in them to make a more or less level floor.

The Lady Raire picked out one for herself, and I helped her clean out the dead leaves and cat droppings and fix up a stone that could be rolled into the opening to block it, in case anything bigger than a woodchuck wanted in. Then she picked out another one and told me it was mine and started in on it. It was dark when we finished. I saw her to her den, then sat down outside it with the pistol in my hand and went to sleep. . . .

—and woke hungry, clear-headed, and wondering how a cat happened to be here, in this super-Mojave. I thought about the dire-beasts and the meat-shredding leeches that had killed Lord Desroy and Sir Orfeo. The cat was no relative of theirs. He had been a regulation-type, black and gray and tan striped feline, complete with vertical-slitted pupils and retractable claws. He looked like anybody's house-cat, except that he was the size of a collie dog. I'd heard about parallel evolution, and I hadn't been too surprised when Sir Orfeo had told me about how many four-legged, one-headed creatures there were in the Universe—but a copy this perfect wasn't possible.

That meant one of two things: Either I had dreamed the whole thing—which was kind of unlikely, inasmuch as when I looked down I saw two more cats, just like the other one, in the bright moonlight down by the water—or our yacht wasn't the first human-owned ship to land on Gar 28.

In the morning light, the water looked clear and inviting. The Lady Raire studied it for a while, then called to me. "Billy Danger, watch thee well the while I lave me. Methinks t'will be safe enow . . ." She glanced my way, and I realized she was talking about going for a swim. I just stared at her.

"How now, art stricken dumb?" she called.

"The pond may be full of poison snakes, crocodiles, quicksand and undertows," I said.

"I'd as lief be devoured as go longer unwashed." She proceeded to unzip the front of the tunic she'd changed into from the temperature suit, and stepped out of it. And for the second time in one minute, I was struck dumb. She stood there in front of me, as naked as a goddess, and as beautiful, and said, "I charge thee, Billy Danger, take not thine eyes from me," and turned and waded down into the water. It was the easiest order to follow I ever heard of.

She stayed in for half an hour, stroking up and down as unconcerned as if she were in the pool at some high-priced resort at Miami Beach. Once or twice she ducked under and stayed so long I found myself wading in to look for her. After the second time I complained and she laughed and promised to stay on top.

"Verily, hast thou found a garden in the wilderness, Billy Danger," she said after she had her clothes back on. " 'Tis so peaceful— and in its rude way, so fair."

"Not much like home, though, I guess, Milady," I said; but she changed the subject, as she always did when the conversation brought back too many memories.

In the next few days, I made two trips back to the car, brought in everything that looked as if it might be useful; then we settled down to what I might describe as a very quiet routine. She strolled around, climbed the rocks, brought home small green shrubs and flowers that she planted around the caves and along the path and watered constantly, using a pot made of clay from the poolside cooked by a Z-gun on wide-beam. I spent my time exploring to the west and north, and trying to make friends with the cats.

There were plenty of them; at certain times of the day, there'd be as many as ten in sight at one time, around the water hole. They didn't pay much attention to us; just watched us when we came toward them and at about fifteen feet, rose casually and moved off into the thick growth along the ravine. They were well fed and lazy, just nice hearthside tabbies, a little larger than usual.

There was one with a few streaks of orange in among the black and tan that I concentrated on, mainly because I could identify him easily. Every time I saw him I'd go out and move up as close as I could without spooking him, sit down, and start to play with a ball of string from the car. He sat and watched. I'd roll it toward him, then pull it back. He moved in closer. I let him get a paw on it, then jerked it. He went after it and cuffed it, and I pulled it in and tossed it out again.

In a week, the game was a regular routine. In two, he had a name—Eureka—and was letting me scratch him between the ears. In three, he had taken to lying across the mouth of my cave, not even moving when I stepped over him going out.

The Lady Raire watched all this with a sort of indulgent smile. According to her, cats were pets on most of the human-inhabited world she knew of. She wasn't sure where they had originated, but she smiled when I said they were a native of Earth.

"In sooth, Billy Danger, 'tis a truism that

each unschooled mind fancies itself the center of the Universe. But the stars were seeded by Man long ago, and by his chattels with him."

At first, the Lady Raire didn't pay much attention to my pet, but one day he showed up limping, and she spent half an hour carefully removing a splinter from his foot. The next day she gave him a bath, and brushed his fur to a high gloss. After that, he took to following her on her walks. And it wasn't long before he took to sleeping at the mouth of her cubbyhole. He got more petting that way.

I watched the cats, trying to see what it was they fed on, on the theory that whatever they ate, we could eat, too. Our concentrates wouldn't last forever. But I never saw them pounce on anything. They came to the water hole to drink and lie around in the shade; then they wandered off again into the undergrowth. One day I decided to follow Eureka.

"As thou wilt," the Lady Raire said, smiling at me. "Tho' I trow thy cat o'mountain lives on naught but moonbeams."

"Baked moonbeam for dinner coming up," I said.

The cat led me up the rocks and through the screen of alien foliage at the north side of the hollow, then struck out along the edge of the ravine, which was filled from edge to edge by a mass of deep-green vines.

The chasm was about three hundred yards long, fifty yards wide; I couldn't see the bottom under the tangle of green, but I could make out the big stems, as thick as my leg, snaking down into the deep shadows for at least a hundred feet. And I could see the cats. They lay in crotches of the big vine, walked delicately along the thick stems, peered out of shadows with green eyes. There were a few up on the rim, sitting on their haunches, watching me watching them. Eureka yawned and switched his tail against my thigh, then made a sudden leap, and disappeared into the green gloom. By getting down on all fours and shading my eyes, I could see the broad branch he'd jumped to. I could have followed, but the idea of going down into that maze full of cats lacked appeal. I got up and started off along the rim. I noticed that it was scattered with what looked like chips of thick eggshell.

The ravine shallowed out to nothing at the far end. The vines were less dense here, and I could see rock strata slanting down into the depths. There were strange knobs and shafts of blackish rock embedded in the lighter stone. I found one protruding near the surface and saw that it was a fossilized bone. The rock was full of them. That would be a matter of deep interest to a paleontologist specializing in the fauna of Gar 28, but it was no help to me. I needed live meat. If there was any around—excepting the cats, and I didn't like the idea of eating them, for six or eight reasons I could think of offhand—it had to be down below, in the shade of the greenery. The descent looked pretty easy, here at the end of the cut. I hitched my gun around front for quick access, and started down.

The rock slanted off under me at an angle of about thirty degrees. The big vines bending up over my head were tough, woody, scaled with dead-looking bark. Only a few green tendrils curled up here, reaching for sunlight. The air was fresh and cool in the shade of the big leaves; there was a sharp, pungent odor of green life, mixed with the rank smell of cat. Fifty feet down the broken slope the growth got too thick to be ignored; it was switch over to limb-climbing or go back. I went on.

It was easy going at first. The stems weren't too close together to push between, and there was still plenty of light to see by. I could hear the cats moving around, back deeper in the growth. I reached a major stem, as big as my torso, and started down it. There were plenty of handholds here. Big seedpods hung in clusters near me. A lot of them had been gnawed, either by the cats or by what the cats ate. So far I hadn't seen any signs of the latter. I broke off one of the pods. It was about a foot long, knobby and pale green. It broke open easily and half a dozen beans as big as egg yolks rolled out. I took a nibble of one. It tasted like raw beans. After a couple of weeks

on concentrates, even that was good—if it
didn't kill me.

I went down. The light was deep green now;
a luminous dusk filtered through a hundred
feet of foliage. The trunk I was following
curved sharply, and I worked my way around
to the up side, descended another ten feet, and
my feet thunked solidly against something
hard. I had to get down on all fours to see that
I was on a smooth, curving surface of tarnished metal.

Something thumped beside me like a dropped blanket; it was Eureka, coming over to
check on me. He sat and washed his face while
I rooted around the base of the big vine, saw
that it was growing out through a fracture in
the metal. The wood had bulged and spread
and shaped itself to conform to the opening. I
had the impression that it was the vine that
had burst the metal.

By crawling, I was able to explore an oval
area about fifteen feet long by ten wide before
the vines slanted in too close to let me move.
All of it was the same iodine-colored metal,
with no seams, no variations in contour, with
the exception of the bulge around the break. If
I wanted to see more, I'd have to do a little
land-clearance. I got out the pistol and set it

on needle-beam, cut enough wood away to get a look into a room the size of a walk-in freezer, almost filled with an impacted growth of wood.

I backed out then, wormed my way over to the big trunk, and climbed back to the surface. There was a lot more to see, but what I wanted to do now was get back in a hurry and tell the Lady Raire that under the vines in the ravine, I'd found a full-sized spaceship.

CHAPTER FOUR

Fifteen minutes later, she stood on the rim of the ravine with me. I could dimly make out the whole three-hundred-foot length of the ship, now that I knew what to look for. It was lying at an angle of about fifteen degrees from the horizontal, the high end to the south.

"It must have been caught by an earthquake," I said. "Or a Garquake."

"I ween full likely she toppled thither," the Lady Raire said. "During a tempest, mayhap. Look thee, where a great fragment has fallen from the rim of the abyss—and see yon broken stones, crushed as she fell."

We found an access route near the south end, well worn by cats, and made an easier approach than my first climb. I led her to the hatch and we spent the next hour burning the

wood away from it, climbed through onto a
floor that slanted down under a tangle of vine
stem to a drift of broken objects half buried in
black dirt at the low end. The air was cool and
damp, and there was a sour smell of rotted
vegetation and stagnant water. We waded
knee-deep in foul-smelling muck to a railed
stair lying on its side, crawled along it to
another open door. I stepped through into a
narrow corridor, and a faint, greenish light
sprang up. I felt the hair stand up on the back
of my neck.

"I misdoubt me not 'tis but an automatic
system," Milady said calmly.

"Still working, after all this time?"

"Why not? 'Twas built to endure." She
pointed to a dark opening in a wall. "Yon
shaft should lead us to the upper decks." She
went past me, and I followed, feeling like a
very small kid in a very large haunted castle.

The shaft led us to a grim-looking place full
of broken piping and big dark shapes the size
of moving vans that Milady said were primi-
tive ion-pulse engines. There was plenty of
breakage visible, but only a few dead tendrils
of vine. We climbed on forward, found a store-
room, a plotting room full of still-shiny equipment, and a lounge where built-in furniture
stuck out from what was now the wall. The
living quarters were on the other side of the
lounge and beyond there was a room with a
ring of dark TV screens arching up overhead
around a central podium that had snapped off

at the base and was hanging by a snarl of conduits. Beyond that point, the nose of the ship was too badly crushed to get into. There were no signs of the original owners, with the possible exception of a few scraps that might have been human bone.

"What do you think, Milady?" I asked her. "Is there anything here we can use?"

"If so, 'twere wonderful, Billy Danger; yet would I see more ere I abandon hope."

Back in the hold, she spent some time crawling over the big vines that came coiling up from somewhere down below.

" 'Tis passing strange," she said. "These stems rise not from soil, but rather burgeon from the bowels of the vessel. And meseemeth they want likeness to the other flora of this world."

I pulled one of the big, leathery leaves over to me. It was heart-shaped, about eight inches wide, strongly ribbed.

"It looks like an ordinary pea to me," I said. "Just overgrown—like the cats."

"We'll trace these to their beginnings, their mystery to resolve." The Lady Raire pointed. "An' mine eyes deceive me not, they rise through yonder hatch."

There was just room to squeeze through between the thigh-thick trunks, into a narrow service shaft. I flashed my light along it, and saw bones.

"Just a cat," I said, more to reassure me than Milady. We went on, ducking under festoons of thick vine. We passed another cat skeleton, well scattered. There was a strange smell, something like crushed almonds with an under-taint of decay. The vines led fifty feet along the passage, then in through a door that had been forced outward off its hinges. The room beyond was a dark mass of coiled white roots. On its far side, faint twilight shone in through a break in the hull. There was a soft clink, like water dripping into a still pond, a faint rustling. I flashed my light down. The floor of the big room slanted off sharply. Down among the snarled roots, a million tiny points of amber light glowed. The Lady Raire took a step back.

"Come, Billy Danger! I like this not—" That was as far as she got before the mass of vine roots in front of me trembled and bulged and all the devils in Hell came swarming out.

Something dirty white, the size of a football, jittering on six spindly legs rushed at me, clicking a pair of jaws that opened sideways in a face like an imp in one of those medieval paintings. I jumped back and swung a kick and its biters clamped onto my boot toe like a steel trap. Another one bounced high enough to rip at my knee; the tough coverall held, but the hide under it tore. Something *zapp*'ed from behind my right ear and a flash of blue fire winked and two of the things skittered away and a stink of burnt horn hit me in the face. All this in the first half-second. I had my pistol up then, squeezing the firing lever, playing it over them like a hose. They curled and jumped and died and more came swarming over the dead ones.

"We're losing," I yelled. "We've got to bottle them up!" The big vine stem was on fire, and sap was bubbling out and spitting in the flames. I ducked down and grabbed up a dead one and threw him into the opening, and beamed another one that poked his snout through and took a step and tripped and went flat on my face. I threw my hands up to protect my head and heard a yowl and something dark bounded across me and there was a snap and a thud and I sat up and saw Eureka, whirling and pouncing, batting with both paws. Behind him the Lady Raire, splashed to the knee with brown, a smear of blood on her cheek, was aiming and firing as steadily as if she were shooting at clay pipes at the county fair. And then Eureka was sitting on his haunches, making a face at me, and the Lady Raire was turning toward me, and there was a last awkward scuffling sound and then silence.

"Well, that answers one question," I said. "Now we know what the cats eat."

It was a hard climb back down along the lift shaft, out through the hold, and up to the last of the sunlight. She got out her belt medikit and started dabbing liquid fire into the cuts on my legs, back, arms and thighs. While she doctored, I talked.

"That was the hydroponics room. When the ship crashed, or fell in the ravine, or got caught in an earthquake, the hull was opened there—or near enough that the plants could sense sunlight. They went for it. Either the equipment that watered them and provided the chemicals they needed was still working, or they found water and soil at the bottom of the ravine; or maybe both. They liked it here; plenty of sunshine, anyway. They adapted and grew and with no competition from other plant life, they developed into what we found."

"There may be truth in thy imaginings, Billy Danger," Milady said. "The vessel's of a very ancient type; 'tis like to those in use on Zeridajh some seven thousand years since."

"That might be long enough for a plant to evolve giant size," I said. "Especially if the local sun puts out a lot of hard radiation. Same for the cats. I guess there were a couple of them aboard—or maybe just one pregnant female. She survived the crash and found water and food—"

"Nay, Billy Danger. Thy Eureka may sup on such dainties as those he slew in they defense—but they'd make two snaps of any house-born puss."

"I didn't mean that; a cat can live on beans, if it has to. Anyway, the critters weren't as big, then."

"How now? Knowest thou the history of Gar's creatures as well as of more familiar kinds?"

"They aren't natives, any more than the cats and the peas. They came along on the trip; to be specific, on the cat."

"Dost rave? Art feverish?"

"I'm ashamed to admit it," I said. "But I know a flea when I see one."

We waited until daylight to go into the ship again. The location of the cat bones gave us a pretty good idea of where the boundaries of flea territory were. Apparently they kept to their dark hold and lived long, happy lives sucking juice from the vines, or an occasional lone cat who meandered over the line. Population pressure drove enough of them upstairs to keep the cats supplied; and the cat droppings and their bodies when they died wound up at the bottom of the ravine, to keep the cycle going.

The Lady Raire had the idea of trying to locate the ship's communication section; she finally did—in the smashed nose section.

I crawled in beside her to look at the ruins of what had once been a message center that could bounce words and music across interstellar distances at a speed that was a complicated multiple of the speed of light. Now it looked like a junkman's nightmare.

"Alack, I deemed I might find here a signaler, intact. 'Twere folly—and yet . . ."

She sounded so downhearted that I had to say something to cheer her up.

"There's an awful lot of gear lying around in there," I said. "Maybe we could salvage something. . . ."

"Dost know aught of these matters, Billy Danger?" she asked in a lofty tone.

"Not much," I said. "I know my way around the inside of an ordinary radio. I'm not talking about sending three-D pictures in glorious color; but maybe a simple signal. . . ."

She wanted to know more. I explained all I'd learned from ICS one summer when I had the idea of Getting Into Radio Now. I felt like an unspoiled native of Borneo explaining flint-chipping techniques to a designer of H-bombs.

It took us a week to assemble a transmitter capable of putting out a simple signal that Milady Raire assured me would show up as a burst of static on any screen within a couple of light-years. We led a big cable from the energy cells that powered the standby lighting system, rigged it so that what juice was in them would drain in one final burst. The ship itself would act as an antenna, once we'd wired our rig to the hull. We climbed out of her, dragging a length of coaxial cable, got back a couple of hundred yards in case of miscalculation with the power core, and touched her off. For a couple of seconds, nothing happened; then later a dull *ka-whoom!* rumbled up from the chasm, followed by a rapid exodus of cats. For the next hour, there was a lot of activity: cats chasing fleas, fleas bouncing around looking for cover, and the Lady Raire and me trying to stay out of the way of both parties. Then the smoke faded away, the fleas scuttled for cover, the cats went back down to lie under the leaves or wandered off in the direction of the water hole, and Milady and I settled down to wait.

I made the discovery that by cutting into a vine just below a leaf, I could get a trickle of cool water. The Lady Raire had the idea of hauling a stem out and getting it growing in the direction of the caves; we did, and it grew enthusiastically. By the time we'd been in residence for another month, we had shade and running water on tap right outside the door.

I asked the Lady Raire to teach me her language, and along with the new words I learned a lot about her home world, Zeridajh. It was old—fifty thousand years of written history—but the men there were still men. It was no classless Utopia where people strolled in misty gardens spouting philosophy; there was plenty of strife and unhappiness, and although the Lady Raire never talked about herself, I got the impression she had her share of the latter. I wondered how it happened that she was off wandering the far end of the Galaxy in the company of two unlikely types like Lord Desroy and Sir Orfeo, but I didn't ask her; if she wanted to tell me, she could. But one day I said something that made her laugh.

"I thought—Sir Orfeo said Lord Desroy had been on Earth three hundred years ago. And you speak the same old-fashioned English—"

She laughed. "Billy Danger, didst deem me so ancient?"

"No—but—"

"I learned my English speech from Lord Desroy, somewhat altered, mayhap, by Sir Orfeo. But 'twas late; indeed, I have but eighteen years, Earth reckoning."

"And you've been away from home for four years? Isn't your family worried . . ." Then I shut up, at the look that crossed her face.

The weather had been gradually changing; the days grew shorter and cooler. The flowers Milady had brought in from the caves dropped their blossoms and turned brown. The cats got restless, and we'd hear them yowling and scrapping, down in their leafy den. And one day, there were kittens everywhere.

Our diet consisted of beans, fried, baked, sliced and eaten raw, chopped and roasted, mixed with food concentrates to make stews and soups. We used the scissors from the first-aid kit to trim our hair back. Fortunately, I had no beard to trim. The days got longer again, and for a while the ravine was a fairyland of blossoms that filled the air with a perfume so sweet it was almost dizzying. At sunset, the Lady Raire would walk out across the desert and look at the purple towers in the west. I trailed her, with a gun ready, in case any of Sir Orfeo's dire-beasts wandered this way.

And one night the ship came.

I was sound asleep; the Lady Raire woke me and I rolled out grabbing for my gun and she pointed to a star that glared blue and got bigger as we watched it. It came down in absolute silence and ground in the desert a quarter of a mile from us in a pool of blue light that cast hard shadows across Milady's face. I was so excited I could hardly breathe, but she wasn't smiling.

"The lines of yon vessel are strange to me, Billy Danger," she said. " 'Tis of most archaic appearance. Seest thou the double hull, like unto the body of an insect?"

"All I can see is the glare from the business end." The blue glow was fading. Big flood-lights came on and lit up the desert all around the ship like high noon.

"Mayhap . . ." she started, and a whistling, whooping noise boomed out across the flats. It stopped and the echoes bounced and faded and it was silent again.

"If 'twere speech, I know it not," Milady said.

"I guess we'd better go meet them," I said, but I had a powerful urge to run and hide among the pea vines.

"Billy Danger, I like this not." Her hand gripped my arm. "Let's flee to the shelter of the ravine—"

Her idea was a little too close to mine; I had to show her how silly her feminine intuition was.

"And miss the only chance we'll ever have to get off this dust-ball? Come on, Milady. You're going home—"

"Nay, Billy—" But I grabbed her arm and advanced. As we came closer, the ship looked as big as a wasp-waisted skyscraper. Three cars came around from the far side of it. Two of them fanned out to right and left; the third headed toward us, laying a dust trail behind it. It was squat, rounded, dark coppery-colored without windows. It stopped fifty feet away with its blunt snout aimed at us. A round panel about a foot in diameter swung open and a glittery assembly poked out and rotated half a turn and was still.

"It looks like it's smelling of us," I said, but the jolly note in my voice was a failure. Then a lid on top popped up like a jack-in-the-box and the most incredible creature I had ever seen climbed out.

He was about four feet high, and almost as wide, and my first impression was that he was a dwarf in Roman armor; then I saw that the armor was part of him. He scrambled down the side of the car on four short, thick legs, then reared his torso up and I got a good look at the face set between a pair of seal flippers in the middle of his chest. It reminded me of a blown-up photo of a bat I'd seen once. There were two eyes, some orifices, lots of wrinkled gray-brown skin, a mouth like a fanged frog. An odd metallic odor came from him. He stared at us and we stared back. Then a patch of rough, pinkish skin centered in a tangle of worms below his face bulged out and a gluey voice came from it. I didn't understand the words, but somehow he sounded cautious.

The Lady Raire answered, speaking too fast for me to follow. I listened while they batted it back and forth. Once she glanced at me and I caught my name and the word "property." I wasn't sure just how she meant it. While they talked, the other two cars came rumbling in from offside, ringing us in.

More of the midgets trotted up, holding what looked like stacks of silver teacups, glued together, the open ends toward us. The spokesman took a step back and made a quick motion of his flippers.

"Throw down guns," he said in Zeridajhi. He didn't sound cautious anymore.

The Lady Raire's hand went toward her pistol. I grabbed her arm.

"I know these hagseed now," she said. "They mean naught but dire mischief to any of my race—"

"Those are gunports under the headlights on the cars," I said. "I think we'd better do what it says."

"If we draw and fire as one—"

"No use, Milady. They've got the drop on us."

She hesitated a moment longer, then unsnapped her gunbelt and let it fall. I did the same. Our new friend made a noise and batted his flippers against the sides, and his gunboys moved in. He pointed at the Lady Raire.

"Fetter this one," he said. "And kill the other."

Two or three things happened at once then. One of the teacup-guns swung my way and the Lady Raire made a sound and threw herself at the gunner. He knocked her down and I charged at him and something exploded in my face and for a long time I slammed against a submerged rock, I heard myself groan, and then I opened my eyes and I was lying on my face with my cheek in a puddle of congealing blood, and the ship and the monsters and the Lady Raire were gone.

For the first few hours my consciousness kept blinking on and off like a defective table lamp. I'd come to and try to move and the next thing I knew I was coming to again. Then suddenly it was daylight, and Eureka was sitting beside me, yowling softly. This time I managed to roll over and raise my head far enough to see myself. I was a mess.

There was blood all over me. I hurt all over, too, so that was no clue. I explored with my hands and found a rip in my coverall along my side, and through that I could feel a furrow wide enough to lay two fingers in. Up higher, there was a hole in my right shoulder that seemed to come out in back; and the side of my neck felt like hamburger, medium rare. The pain wasn't really as bad as you'd expect. I must have been in shock. I flopped back and listened to all the voices around me. I heard Sir Orfeo: *She's your responsibility now, Jongo. Take care of her.*

"I tried," I said. "I really tried—"

It's all right, the Lady Raire was standing by me, looking scared, but smiling at me. *I trust you, Billy Danger.* The light from the open furnace door glowed in her black hair, and she turned and stepped into the flames and I yelled and reached after her, but the fires leaped up and I was awake again, sobbing.

"They've got her," I said aloud. "She was frightened of them, but I had to show off. I led her out to them like a lamb to the slaughter. ..." I pictured her, dragged aboard the dwarf's ship, locked away in a dark place, alone and terrified, and with no one to help her. And she trusted me. . . .

"My fault," I groaned. "My fault! But don't be afraid, Milady. I'll find you. They think I'm dead, but I'll trick them; I won't die. I'll stay alive, and find them and take you home. . . ."

The next time I was aware of what was going on, the cat was gone and the sun was directly overhead and I was dying of thirst. By turning my head, I could see the vines along the edge of the ravine. There was shade there, and water. I got myself turned over on my stomach and started crawling. It was a long trip—nearly a hundred yards—and I passed out so many times I lost count. But I reached the vines and got myself a drink and then it was dark. That meant it had been about seventy-two hours since the slug-people had done such a sloppy job of killing me. I must have slept for a long time, then. When I woke up, Eureka was back, with a nice fresh flea for me.

"Thanks, boy," I said when he dropped the gift on my chest and nudged me with his nose. "It's nice to know somebody cares."

"You're not dead yet," he said, and his voice sounded like Orfeo's. I called to him, but he was gone, down into the darkness. I followed him, along a trail of twisted vines, but the light always glimmered just ahead, and I was cold and wet and then the fleas came swarming out on the empty eyes of a giant skull and swarmed over me and I felt them eating me alive and I woke up, and I was still there, under the vines, and my wounds were hurting now and Eureka was gone and the flea with him.

I got myself up on all fours to have another drink from the water vine, and noticed a young bean pod sprouting nearby. I was hungry and I tore it open and ate the beans. And the next time I woke up, I was stronger.

For five long Garish days I stayed under the vines; then I made the trek to the caves. After that, on a diet of concentrates, I gained strength faster. I spent my time exercising my wounds so they wouldn't stiffen up too much as they healed, and talking to the cat. He didn't answer me anymore, so I judged I was getting better. No infections set in; the delousing Sir Orfeo had given me probably had something to do with that, plus the absence of microbes on Gar 28.

Finally a day came when it was time to get out and start seeing the world again. I slung my crater-rifle, not without difficulty, since my right arm didn't want to cooperate, and made a hike around the far side of the ravine, with half a dozen rest stops. I was halfway back to the hut and the drink of water I'd promised myself as a reward, when the second ship came.

CHAPTER FIVE

This one was smaller, something like Lord Orfeo's yacht, but with less of a polish. I hid behind the vines with my gun aimed until I saw what were undoubtedly Men emerge. Then I went up to meet them.

They were small, yellow-skinned, with round, bald heads. The captain was named Ancu-Uriru and he spoke a little Zeridajhi. He frowned at my scars, which were pretty spectacular, and wanted to know where the rest of the ship's complement were. I told him there was just me. That made him frown worse than ever. It seemed he had picked up our signal and answered it in the hope of collecting a nice reward from somebody, along with a little salvage. I told him about the ship in the ravine, and he sent a couple of men down who came back shaking their heads. They showed every sign of being ready to leave then.

"What about me?" I asked Ancu-Uriru.

"We leave you in peace," he said in an off-hand way.

"There's such a thing as too much peace," I told him. "I want to go with you. I'll work my way."

"I have no need of you; space is limited aboard my small vessel. And I fear your wounds render you somewhat less than capable to perform useful labor. Here you are more comfortable. Stay, with my blessing."

"Suppose I told you where there was another ship, a luxury model, in perfect shape—if you can get the doors open?"

That idea seemed to strike a spark. We dickered for a while, and there were hints that a little torture might squeeze the answers out of me with no need for favors in return. But in the end we struck a deal: My passage to a civilized port in return for Lord Desroy's yacht.

It took them most of a Garish day to trickle her locks open. Ancu-Uriru looked her over, then ordered his personal effects moved into the owner's suite. I was assigned to ride on his old tub along with a skeleton crew. Just before boarding time, Eureka came bounding across the flats toward me. One of the men had a gun in his hand, and I jumped in front of him just in time.

"This is my cat," I told him. "He saved my

life. We used to have long talks, while I was sick."

The men all seemed to be cat-lovers; they gathered around and admired him.

"Bring the beast along," Ancu-Uriru said. We went aboard then, and an hour later the ship lifted off Gar 28, as nearly as I could calculate, one year after I had landed.

It wasn't a luxury cruise. The man Ancu-Uriru had assigned to captain the tub—In-Ruhic, by name—believed in every man's working his way, in spite of the generous fare I'd paid. Even aboard as sophisticated a machine as a spaceship, there was plenty of coolie labor, as I well remembered from my apprenticeship under Sir Orfeo. The standards he'd taught me carried over here; after my assigned chores were done, I spent long hours chipping and scraping and cleaning and polishing, trying single-handed to clear away grime that had been accumulating since the days of the Vikings—or longer. According to In-Ruhic, the old ship had been built on a world called Urhaz, an unknown number of millenia ago.

At first, my wounds caused me a lot of pain, until In-Ruhic stopped me one day and told me my groans were interfering with his inward peace. He had me stretch out on a table while he rubbed some vile-smelling grease into the scars.

"How you survived, untended, is a matter of wonder," he said. "I think you lost a pound of flesh and bone here, where the pellet tore through your shoulder. And you've broken ribs, healed crookedly. And your throat! Man, under the web of scar tissue, I can see the pulse of the great vein each time you lift your chin!" But his hands were as gentle as any girl's could have been; he gave me a treatment every day for a few weeks. The glop he used must have had some healing effect because the skin toughened up over the scars and the pain gradually faded.

I told In-Ruhic and the others about the wasp-waisted ship and the armored midgets that had taken the Lady Raire; but they'd never seen or heard of their kind. They wagged their heads and grunted in vicarious admiration when I described her to them.

"But these are matters best forgotten, Biri-danju—" that was as close as In-Ruhic seemed to be able to get to my name. "I've heard of the world called Zeridajh; distant it is, and inhabited by men as rich as emperors. Doubt-less these eve-doers you tell of have long since sold her there for ransom."

By the time the world where Ancu-Uriru planned to drop me was visible in the view-screen on the bridge where I was pulling watches as a sort of assistant instrument reader, I was almost a full-fledged member of the crew. Just before we started our landing maneuvers, which were more complicated for an old tub like In-Ruhic's command than they had been for Lord Desroy's ultramodern yacht, In-Ruhic took me aside and asked me what my plans were.

"If there's a Zeridajhi Embassy, I'll go there and tell them about the Lady Raire. Or maybe I can send some kind of message through. If not . . . well, I'll figure out something."

He shook his head and looked sad and wise. "You nurture a hopeless passion for this high-born lady," he started.

"Nothing like that," I cut him off short. "She was in my care. I'm responsible."

He put a hand on my shoulder. "Biridanju, you've shown yourself a willing worker, and quick to learn. Stay on with me. I offer you a regular berth aboard this vessel."

"Thanks, In-Ruhic. But I have another job to do."

"Think well, Biridanju. For a foreigner, work is not easy to find; and to shore folk, who know not the cruel ways of space, your little decorations may prove unsightly, an added incubus."

I put a hand up and felt the lumps and ridges along the side of my throat and jaw. "I know; it looks like hell. But I'm not asking for any beauty prizes. I'll pay my way."

"I suppose you must make your try. But after, Biridanju—remember: We're based nearby, and call here at Inciro ever and anon. I'll welcome you as shipmate whenever you're ready."

We landed a few hours later on a windswept ramp between a gray sea and a town growing on a hillside. Captain Ancu-Uriru was there ahead of us. He talked earnestly with In-Ruhic for a while, then invited me to his quarters aboard the yacht. There he sat me down and offered me a drink and a double-barreled cigar, rolled from two different weeds which, when combined, produced a smoke worse than any three nickle stogies.

"Biridanju, I tell you freely, you've made me a rich man," he said. "I thought at first you were a shill who'd bring pirates down on me. Almost, I had you shot before you boarded." He made a face that might have been a smile. "Your cat saved you. It passed reason that a man with your wounds, *and* an animal-lover, could be but a decoy for corsairs. I ordered In-Ruhic to watch you closely, and for long I slept but little, watching these beautiful screens for signs of mischief. Now I know I did you an injury."

"You saved my life," I said. "No apologies needed."

He lifted a flat box from a drawer of the gorgeous inlaid desk. "I am a just man, Biridanju; or so I hope. I sold the special stores aboard this cutter for a sum greater than any year's profits I've known since I first captained a trader. The proceeds are yours, your fair share."

I lifted the lid and looked at an array of little colored sticks an eighth of an inch square and an inch long.

"There is enough there to keep you in comfort for many years," he said. "If you squander it not on follies, such as star-messages or passenger fares—not that there's enough to take you far." He gave me a sharp look that meant In-Ruhic had told him my plans.

I thanked him and assured him I'd make it go as far as I could.

It took me ten minutes to collect my personal belongings from the ship and buckle Eureka into the harness I'd made for him. Then Ancu-Uriru took me through the port formalities, which weren't much for anyone with a bankroll, and found me an inn in the town. In-Ruhic joined us for a final drink in my room, and then they left, and I sat on the side of the plain little bunk in the plain little room in the yellow twilight and scratched Eureka behind the ears and felt the loneliness close in.

The town was named Inciro, like the planet.

It was one of half a dozen ports that had been built ages past to handle the long-vanished trade in minerals and hides and timber from the interior of the one big continent. The population of about ten thousand people, many of whom had six fingers on each hand for some reason, were tall, dark-eyed, pale-skinned, gloomy-looking, with a sort of Black Irish family resemblance, like Eskimos or Hottentots. I spent a few days wandering around the town, sampling the food in different chophouses and seafood dives—they were all good—and drinking a tasty red beer called "izm." The mix dialect I'd learned from In-Ruhic and his men was good enough to carry on a basic conversation. I sooned learned there was no Zeridajhi Embassy anywhere on the planet; the nearest thing to it was a consular agent representing the commercial interest of the half dozen worlds within five light-years of Inciro.

I called on him. He was a fattish, hairy man in a stale-smelling office over a warehouse. He steepled his pudgy fingers and listened to what I had to say, then solemnly suggested I forgot the whole thing. It seemed it was a big Galaxy, and the things that had maimed me and stolen Milady Raire could be anywhere in it—probably at the far side of it by now. No belligerent nonhuman had been seen in these parts for more centuries than I had years. He would have liked to have told me I'd imagined it all, but his eyes kept straying back to my scars.

Eureka went with me on my walks, attracting quite a bit of attention at first. The Incirinos had seen a few cats before, but none his size. He did more than keep me company; one evening a trio of roughnecks with too many bowls of izm inside them came over to get a closer look at my scars, and he came to his feet from where he'd been curled up under the table and made a sound like tearing canvas and showed a mouthful of teeth, and they backed away fast.

I found a little old man who hung around one of the bars who knew half a dozen useful dialects. For the price of enough drinks each evening to keep him in a talking mood, he gave me language lessons, plus the beginnings of an education on the state of this end of the Galaxy. He told me how the human race had developed a long time ago on a world near Galactic Center, had spread outward in all directions for what must have been a couple of hundred thousand years, settled every habitable planet they found and built a giant empire that collapsed peacefully after a while of its own weight. That had been over twenty thousand years earlier; and since then the many separate tribes of Man had gone their own ways.

"Now, take you," he poked a skinny finger at me. "From a planet you call 'Eart.' Thought you were the only people in the Universe. But all you were was a passed-over colony, or maybe what was left of a party marooned by an accident; or a downed battleship. Or maybe you were a penal colony. Or perhaps a few people wandered out there, just wanting to be alone. A few thousand years pass, and—there you are!" He looked triumphant, as if he'd just delivered a rigorous proof of the trisection of the angle.

"But we've dug up bones," I told him. "Apemen, and missing links. They show practically the whole chain of evolution, from animals to men. And we've got gorillas and chimps and monkeys that look too much like us to just be coincidence."

"Who said anything about coincidence?" he came back. "Life adapts to conditions. Similar conditions, similar life. You ever look at the legs and feet on plink-lizard? Swear they were human, except they're only so long. Look at flying creatures; birds, mammals, reptiles, goranos, or mikls; they all have wings, all flap 'em, all have hollow bones, use two legs for walking—"

"Even Eureka here is related to humanity," I pressed on. "We have more similarities than we have differences. As embryos of a few weeks, you can't tell us apart."

He nodded and grinned. "Uh-huh. And where'd you say you got him? Not on Eart."

It was like arguing religion. Talking about it just confirmed everyone in his original opinion. But the talking was good experience. By the time I'd been on Inciro for three months, Earth time, I was fluent in the lingua franca that the spacers used, and had a pretty good working vocabulary in a couple of other dialects. And I kept my Zeridajhi sharpened up with long imaginary conversations with the Lady Raire, in which I explained over and over again how we *should* have greeted the midgets.

I looked up a local surgeon who examined by wounds and clucked and after a lot of lab studies and allergy tests, put me under an anesthetic and rebuilt my shoulder with metal and plastic to replace what was missing. When the synthetic skin had stitched itself in with the surrounding hide, he operated again, to straighten out my ribs. He wanted to re-upholster the side of my neck and my jaw next, but the synthetic hide was the same pale color as the locals; it wouldn't have improved my looks much. And by then, I was tired of the pain and boredom of plastic surgery. My arm worked all right now, and I could stand straight again instead of cradling my smashed side. And it was time to move on.

In-Ruhic's ship called about then, and I asked his advice.

"I don't want to sign on for just a local run," I told him. "I want to work my way toward Zeridajh, and ask questions along the way. Sooner or later I'll find a lead to the midgets."

"This is a long quest you set yourself, Biri-

danju," he said. "And a vain one." But he took
me along to a local shipowner and got me a
place as an apprentice powersection tender
on a freighter bound inward toward a world
called Topaz.

Eureka and I saw Topaz, and after that
Greu and Poylon and Trie and Pandache's
World and the Three Moons. Along the way, I
learned the ins and outs of an ion-pulse drive
and a stressed-field generator; and I served
my time in vac suits, working outside under
the big black sky that wrapped all the way
around and seemed to pull at me like a mag-
net that would suck me away into its deepest
blackest depths, every hour I spent out on a
hull.

And I had my head pounded by a few fore-
castle strongarm types, until an oak-tough old
tube-man who'd almost been fleet champion
once in his home-world's navy showed me a
few simple tricks to keep from winding up on
the short end of every bout. His method was
effective: he pounded me harder than the
bully-boys until I got fast enough to bloody
his nose one night, and graduated.

I learned to pull duty three on, three off, to
drink the concoctions that space-faring men
seemed to always be able to produce no

matter how far they were from the last port, and to play seventy-one different games with hundred-and-four card decks whose history was lost in antiquity. And at every world I asked, and got the same answer: No such animals as the midgets had been seen in five thousand years and probably not then.

On a world called Unriss, in a library that was a museum relic itself, I found a picture of a midget—or a reasonable facsimile. I couldn't read the text, but the librarian could make out a little of the old language. It said the thing was called a H'eeaq, that it was a denizen of a world of the same name, and that it was extinct. Where H'eeaq was located, it neglected to say.

My small bankroll, which would have kept me in modest circumstances on Inciro, didn't last long. I spent it carefully, item by item outfitted my chest, including a few luxuries like a dreamer and a supply of tapes, a good power gun, and shore clothes. I studied astrogation and power section maintenance whenever I was able to get hold of a tape I hadn't seen before. By the time two years had passed, I had been promoted to power chief, second class, meaning I was qualified to act as standby chief on vessels big enough to have a standby complement. That was a big step forward —like jumping from Chinese junks to tramp steamers. It meant I could ship on bigger, faster vessels, with longer range.

I reached a world called Lhiza after a six

months' cruise on a converted battle cruiser, and spent three months on the beach there, spending my back pay on new training tapes and looking for a berth that would take me into the edge of the sector of the Galaxy known as the Bar. It wasn't easy; few of the older, slower hulls that worked the Eastern Arm had business there. But the Bar was where Zeridajh was, still thousands of light-years away, but getting closer.

The vessel I finally shipped on was a passenger liner, operating under a contract with the government of a world called Ahaz, hauling immigrant labor. I didn't much like the idea; it was my first time nursemaiding a shipload of Flatlanders. But I was offered a slot as first powerman, and the tub *was* going a long way, and in the right direction. So I signed on.

She was an old ship, like most of the hulls operating in the Arm, but she had been a luxury job in her day. I had a suite to myself, with room for Eureka, so for the first time aboard ship the old cat got to sleep across my feet, the way he did ashore. The power section was a massive, old-fashioned stressed-field installation; but after the first few weeks of shakedown and impressing my ideas on my crew I had the engines running smoothly. Everything settled down then to the quiet, slightly dull, sometimes pleasant, always monotonous routine that all long cruises are.

My first shift chief, Ommu, was a big-muscled, square-faced fellow with the faint green-ish cast to his skin that said he was from a high Co world. He listened to my story of the midgets, and told me that once, many years before, he'd seen a similar ship, copper-color-ed. It had drifted into a cometary orbit around a world in the Guree system, in the Bar. She was a navigational hazard and he'd been one of the crew assigned to rendezvous with her and set vaporizing charges. Against standing orders, he and another sapper had crawled in through a hole in her side to take a look around. The ship had been long dead, and there wasn't much left of the crew; but he had picked up a souvenir. He got it from his ship chest and laid it on the mess table in front of me. It looked like a stack of demitasse cups, dull silver, with a loop at the base and a short rod projecting from the open end.

"Yeah," I said, and felt my scalp prickle, just looking at it. It wasn't identical with the guns that had shot me up, back on Gar 28, but it was a close enough relative.

I had him tell me all about the ship, every-thing he could remember. There wasn't much. We went up to the ship's psychologist and after a lot of persuasion and a bottle of crude stuff frm the power-section still, he agreed to run a recall on Ommu under hypnosis. I checked with the purser and located a xenolo-gist among the passengers, and got him to sit in on the session.

In a light trance, Ommu relived the approach to the ship, described it in detail as he came up on it from sun-side. We followed him inside, through the maze of compartments; we were with him as he stirred the remains of what must have been a H'eeaq and turned up the gun.

The therapist ran him back through in three times, and he and the xenologist took turns firing questions at him. At the end of two hours, Ommu was soaking wet and I had the spooky feeling I'd been aboard that derelict with him.

The xenologist wanted to go back to his quarters and pore over his findings, but I talked him into giving us a spot analysis of what he'd gotten.

"The vessel itself appears a typical artifact of what we call the H'eeaq Group," he said. "They are an echinodermoid form, originating far out in Fringe Space, or, as some have theorized, representing an incursion from a neighboring stellar assemblage, presumably the Lesser Cloud. Their few fully documented contacts with Man, and with other advanced races of the Galaxy, reveal a cultural pattern of marked schizoid-accretional character—"

"Maybe you could make that a little plainer," Ommu sugested.

"There are traits reflecting a basic disintegration of the societal mechanism," he told us, and elaborated on that for a while. The simplified explanation was as bad as the regular one, as far as my vocabulary was concerned. I told him so.

"Look here," he snapped. He was a peppery little man. "You're asking me to extrapolate from very scanty data, to place my professional reputation in jeopardy—"

"Nothing like that, sir," I soothed him. "I'd just like to have a little edge the next time I meet those types."

"Ummm. There's their basic insecurity, of course. I'd judge their home-world has been cataclysmically destroyed, probably the bulk of their race along with it. What this might do to a species with a strong racial-survival drive is anyone's guess. If I were you, I'd look for a complex phobia system: Fear of heights or enclosed spaces, assorted fetish symbologies. And of course, the bully syndrome. Convince them you're stronger, and they're your slaves. Weaker, and they destroy you."

That was all I got from him. Ommu gave me the teacup gun. I disassembled it and examined its workings, but it didn't tell me much. The routine closed in again then. I fine-tuned the generators, and put the crew on polishing until the section gleamed from one end to the other. I won some money playing tikal, lost it again at revo. And then one off-shift I was shocked up out of a deep sleep to find myself lying on the floor, with Eureka yowling over me and every alarm bell on the ship screaming disaster.

By the time I reached the power section, the buffeting was so bad that I had to grab a rail to stay on my feet.

"I've tried to get through to Command for orders," Ommu yelled over the racket, "but no contact!"

I tried the interdeck screen, raised a young plotman with blood on his face who told me the whole forward end of the ship had been carried away by a collision, with what, he didn't know. That was all he told me before the screen blanked in the middle of a word.

A new shock knocked both of us down. The deck heaved up under us and kept going, right on up and over.

"She's tumbling," I yelled to Ommu. "She'll break up, fast, under this! Order the men to lifeboat stations!" A tubeman named Rusi showed up then, pale as chalk, hugging internal injuries. I gave him a hand and we crawled on floors, walls and ceilings, made it to our boat station. The bay door was blown wide and the boat was hanging in its davits with the stern torn out, and there were pieces of a dead man scattered around. I ordered the men up to the next station and started to help my walking wounded, but he was dead.

The upper bay was chaos. I grabbed a gun from a lanky grandpa who was waving it and yelling, and fired over the crowd. Nobody noticed. Ommu joined me, and with a few crewmen, we formed up a flying wedge. Ommu got the hatch open while the rest of us beat back the mob. All this time, Eureka had stayed close to me, with his ears flattened and his tail twitching.

"Take 'em in order," I told Ommu. "Anybody tries to walk over somebody else, I'll shoot him!" Two seconds later I had to make that good when a beefy two-hundred-pounder charged me. I blew a hole through him and the rest of them scattered back. The boat had been designed for fifty passengers; we had eighty-seven aboard when a wall of fire came rolling down the corridor and Ommu grabbed me just in time and hauled me in across the laps of a fat woman and a middle-aged man who was crying, and Eureka bounded in past me. I got forward and threw in the big red lever and a big boot kicked us and then there was the sick, null-G feel that meant we'd cleared the launch tube and were on our own.

In the two-by-four Command compartment, I watched the small screen where five miles away the ship was rotating slowly, end-over-end, with debris trailing off from her in a lazy spiral. Flashes of light sparkled at points along the hull where smashed piping was spewing explosive mixtures. Her back broke and the aft third of the ship separated and a cloud of tiny objects, some of them human, scattered out into the void, exploding as they hit vacuum. The center section blew then, and when the smoke cleared, there was nothing left but a major fragment of the stern, glowing redhot, and an expanding dust-cloud.

"Any other boats get away?" I asked.

"I didn't see any, Billy."

"There were five thousand people aboard that scow! We can't be the only survivors!" I yelled at him, as if convincing him would make it true.

A power man named Lath stuck his head in. "We've got some casualties back here," he said. "Where in the Nine Hells are we, anyway?"

I checked the chart screen. The nearest world was a planet named Cyoc, blue-coded, which meant uninhabited and uninhabitable.

"Nothing there but a beacon," Ommu said. "An ice world."

We checked; found nothing within a year's range that was any better—or as good.

"Cyoc it is," I said. "Now let's take a look at what we've got to work with."

I led the way down the no-G central tube past the passenger cells that were arranged radially around it, like the kernels on a corn-cob. They were badly overcrowded. There seemed to be a lot of women and children. Maybe the mob had demonstrated some of the chivalric instincts, after all; or maybe Ommu had done some selecting I didn't notice. I wasn't sure he'd done the right thing.

A big man, wearing what had been expensive clothes before the mob got to them, pushed out in the aisle up ahead of me, waited for me to come to him.

"I'm Till Ognath, member of the Ahacian Assembly," he stated. "As highest ranking individual aboard, I'm assuming command. I see you're crew; I want you men to run a scan of the nearby volume of space and give me a choice of five possible destinations within our cruise capability. Then—"

"This is Chief Danger, Power Section," Ommu butted into his spiel. "He's ranking crew."

Assemblyman Ognath looked me over. "Better give me the gun." He held out a broad, well tended hand.

"I'll keep it," I said. "I'll be glad to have your help, Assemblyman."

"Maybe I didn't make myself clear," Ognath showed me a well-bred frown. "As a member of the World Assembly of Ahax, I—"

"Ranking crew member assumes command, Assemblyman," Ommu cut him off. "Better crawl back in your hole, Mister, before you qualify yourself for proceedings under space law."

"You'd quote law to me, you—" Ognath's vocabulary failed him.

"I'll let you know how you can best be of service, Assemblyman," I told him, and we moved on and left him still looking for a suitable word.

The boat was in good shape, fully equipped and supplied—for fifty people, all of whom were presumed to have had plenty of time to pack and file aboard like ladies and gentlemen. Assemblyman Ognath made a formal complaint about the presence of an animal aboard, but he was howled down. Everybody seemed to think a mascot was lucky. Anyway, Eureka ate very little and took up no useful space. Two of the injured died the first day, three more in the next week. We put them out the lock and closed ranks.

There wasn't much room for modesty aboard, for those with strong feelings about such matters. One man objected to another man's watching his wife taking a sponge bath—(ten other people were watching, too; they had no choice in the matter, unless they screwed their eyes shut) and knocked his front teeth out with a belt-buckle. Two days later, the jealous one turned up drifting in the no-G tube with his windpipe crushed. Nobody seemed to miss him much, not even the wife.

Two hundred and sixty-nine hours after we'd kicked free of the foundering ship, we were maneuvering for an approach to Cyoc. From five hundred miles up, it looked like one huge snowball.

It was my first try at landing an atmosphere boat. I'd run through plenty of drills, but the real thing was a little different. Even with fully automated controls that only needed a decision made for them here and there along the way, there were still plenty of things to do wrong. I did them all. After four hours of the roughest ride this side of a flatwheeled freight car, we slammed down hard in a mountain-rimmed icefield something over four hundred miles from the beacon station.

CHAPTER SIX

The rough landing had bloodied a few noses, one of them mine, broken an arm or two, and opened a ten-foot seam in the hull that let in a blast of refrigerated air; but that was incidential. The real damage was to the equipment compartment forward. The power plant had been knocked right through the side of the boat. That meant no heat, no light, and no communications. Assemblyman Ognath told me what he thought of my piloting ability. I felt pretty bad until Ommu got him to admit he knew even less about atmosphere flying than I did.

The outside temperature was ten below freezing; that made it a warm day, for Cyoc. The sun was small and a long way off, glaring in a dark, metallic sky. It shed a sort of gray,

before-the-storm light over a hummocky
spread of glacier that ended at blue peaks,
miles away. Assemblyman Ognath told me
that now we were on terra firma he was
taking charge, and that we would waste no
time taking steps for rescue. He didn't say
what steps. I told him I'd retain command as
long as the emergency lasted. He fumed and
used some strong language, but I was still
wearing the gun.

There were a lot of complaints from the
passengers about the cold, the short rations,
the recycled water, bruises, and other things.
They'd been all right, in space, glad to be
alive. Now that they were ashore they seemed
to expect instant relief. I called some of the
men aside for a conference.

"I'm taking a party to make the march to
the beacon," I told them.

"Party?" Ognath bellied up to me. "We'll all
go! Only by pulling together can we hope to
survive!"

"I'm taking ten men," I said. "The rest stay
here."

"You expect us to huddle here in this wreck,
and slowly freeze to death?" Ognath wanted
to know.

"Not you, Assemblyman," I said. "You're
coming with me."

He didn't like that, either. He said his place
was with the people.

"I want the strongest, best-fed men," I said.
"We'll be traveling with heavy packs at first. I
can't have stragglers."

"Why not just yourself, and this fellow?" Ognath jerked a thumb at Ommu.

"We're taking half the food with us. Somebody has to carry it."

"Half the food—for ten men? And you'd leave seventy-odd women and children to share what's left?"

"That's right. We'll leave now. There's still a few hours of daylight."

Half an hour later we were ready to go, the cat included. The cold didn't seem to bother him. The packs were too big by half, but they'd get lighter.

"Where's your pack, Danger?" Ognath wanted to know.

"I'm not carrying one," I told him. I left the boat in charge of a crewman with a sprained wrist; when I looked back at the end of the first hour all I could see was ice.

We made fifteen miles before sunset. When we camped, several of the men complained about the small rations, and a couple mentioned the food I gave Eureka. Ognath made another try to gather support for himself as trail boss, but without much luck. We turned in and slept for five hours. It wasn't daylight yet when I rolled them out. One man complained that his suit-pack was down; he was shivering, and blue around the lips. I sent him back and distributed his pack among the others.

We went on, into rougher country, sprinkled with rock slabs that pushed up through the ice. The ground was rising, and footing was treacherous. When I called the noon halt, we had made another ten miles.

"At this rate, we'll cover the distance in ten days," Ognath informed me. "The rations could be doubled, easily! We're carrying enough for forty days!"

He had some support on that point. I said no. After a silent meal and a ten-minute rest, we went on. I watched the men. Ognath was a complainer but he held his position up front. Two men had a tendency to straggle. One of them seemed to be having trouble with his pack. I checked on him, found he had a bad bruise on his shoulder from a fall during the landing. I chewed him out and sent him back to the boat.

"If anybody else is endangering this party by being noble, speak up now," I told them. Nobody did. We went on, down to eight men already, and only twenty-four hours out.

The climbing was stiff for the rest of the day. Night caught us halfway to a high pass. Everybody was dog-tired. Ommu came over and told me the packs were too heavy.

"They'll get lighter," I told him.

"Maybe if you carried one you'd see it my way," he came back.

"Maybe that's why I'm not carrying one."

We spent a bad night in the lee of an ice-ridge. I ordered all suits set for minimum heat to conserve power. At dawn we had to dig ourselves out of drifted snow.

We made the pass by mid-afternoon, and were into a second line of hills by dark. Up until then, everyone had been getting by on his initial charge; now the strain was starting to show. When morning came, two men had trouble getting started. After the first hour, one of them passed out cold. I left him and the other fellow with a pack between them, to make it back to the boat. By dark, we'd put seventy-five miles behind us.

I began to lose track of days then. One man slipped on a tricky climb around a crevasse and we lost him, pack and all. That left five of us: myself, Ommu, Ognath, a passenger named Choom, and Lath, one of my power-section crew. Their faces were hollow and when they pulled their masks off their eyes looked like wild animals'; but we'd weeded out the weak ones now.

At a noonday break, Ognath watched me passing out the ration cans.

"I thought so," his fruity baritone was just a croak now. "Do you men see what he's doing?" He turned to the others, who had sprawled on their backs as usual as soon as I called the halt. "No wonder Danger's got more energy than the rest of us! He's giving himself double rations—for himself and the animal!"

They all sat up and stared my way.

"How about it?" Ommu asked. "Is he right?"

"Never mind me," I told them. "Just eat and get what rest you can. We've still got nearly three hundred miles to do."

Ommu got to his feet. "Time you doubled up on rations for all of us," he said. The other two men were sitting up, watching.

"I'll decide when it's time," I told him.

"Ognath, open a pack and hand out an extra ration all around," Ommu said.

"Touch a pack and I'll kill you," I said. "Lie down and get your rest, Ommu."

They stood there and looked at me.

"Better be careful how you sleep from now on, Danger," Ommu said. Nobody said anything while we finished eating and shouldered packs and started on. I marched at the rear now, watching them. I couldn't afford to let them fail. The Lady Raire was counting on me.

At the halfway point, I was still feeling fairly strong. Ognath and Choom had teamed up to help each other over the rough spots, and Ommu and Lath stuck together. None of them said anything to me unless they had to. Eureka had taken to ranging far offside, looking for game, maybe.

Each day's march was like the one before. We got on our feet at daylight, wolfed down a ration, and hit the trail. Our best speed was about two miles per hour now. The scenery never changed. When I estimated we'd done two hundred and fifty miles—about the fifteenth day—and I increased the ration. We made better time that day, and the next. Then the pace began to drag again. The next day, there were a lot of falls. It wasn't just rougher ground; the men were reaching the end of their strength. We halted in mid-afternoon and I told them to turn their suit heaters up to medium range. I saw Ognath and Choom swap looks. I went over to the assemblyman and checked his suit; it was on full high. So was Choom's.

"Don't blame them, Danger," Ommu said. "On short rations they were freezing to death."

The next day Choom's heat-pack went out. He kept up for an hour; then he fell and couldn't get up. I checked his feet; they were frozen waxy-white, ice-hard, halfway to the knee.

We set up a tent for him, left fourteen days' ration, and went on. Assemblyman Ognath told me this would be one of the items I'd answer for at my trial.

"Not unless we reach the beacon," I reminded him.

Two days later, Ognath jumped me when he thought I was asleep. He didn't know I had scattered ice chips off my boots around me as a precaution. I woke up just in time to roll out of his way. He rounded and came for me again and Eureka knocked him down and stood over him, snarling in a way to chill your blood. Lath and Ommu heard him yell and I had to hold the gun on them to get them calmed down.

"Rations," Ognath said. "Divide them up now; four even shares!"

I turned him down. Ommu told me what he'd do to me as soon as he caught me without the gun. Lath asked me if I was willing to kill the cat, now that it had gone mad and was attacking people. I let them talk. When they had it out of their systems, we went on. That afternoon Ommu fell and couldn't get up. I took his pack and told Lath to help him. An hour later Lath was down. I called a halt, issued a triple ration all around and made up what was left of the supplies into two packs. Ognath complained, but he took one and I took the other.

The next day was a hard one. We were into broken ground again, and Ognath was having trouble with his load, even though it was a lot lighter than the one he'd started with. Ommu and Lath took turns helping each other up. Sometimes it was hard to tell which one was helping which. We made eight miles and pitched camp. The next day we did six miles; the next five; the day after that, Ognath fell and sprained an ankle an hour after we'd started. By then we had covered three hundred and sixty miles.

"We'll make camp here," I said. "Ommu and Lath, lend a hand."

I used the filament gun on narrow-beam to cut half a dozen foot-cube blocks of snow. When I told Ommu to start stacking them in a circle, he just looked at me.

"He's gone crazy," he said. "Listen, Lath; you too, Ognath. We've got to rush him. He can't kill three of us—"

"We're going to build a shelter," I told him. "You'll stay warm there until I get back."

"What are you talking about?" Lath was hobbling around offside, trying to get behind me. I waved him back.

"This is the end of the line for you. Ognath can't go anywhere; you two might make another few miles, but the three of you together will have a better chance."

"Where do you think you're going?" Ognath got himself up on one elbow to call out. "Are you abandoning us now?"

"He planned it this way all along," Lath whispered. His voice had gone a couple of days before. "Made us pack his food for him, used us as draft animals; and now that we're used up, he'll leave us here to die."

Ommu was the only one who didn't spend the next ten minutes swearing at me. He flopped down on the snow and watched me range the snow blocks in a ten-foot circle. I cut and carried up more and built the second course. When I had the third row in place, he got up and silently started chinking the gaps with snow.

It took two hours to finish the igloo, including a six-foot entrance tunnel and a sanitary trench a few feet away.

"We'll freeze inside that," Ognath was almost blubbering now. "When our suit-packs go, we'll freeze!"

I opened the packs and stacked part of the food, made up one light pack.

"Look," Ognath was staring at the small heap of ration cans. "He's leaving us with nothing! We'll starve, while he stuffs his stomach!"

"If you starve you won't freeze," I said. "Better get him inside," I told Ommu and Lath.

"He won't be stuffing his stomach much," Ommu said. "He's leaving us twice what he's taking for himself."

"But—where's all the food he's been hoarding?"

"We've been eating it for the past week," Ommu said. "Shut up, Ognath. You talk too much."

We put Ognath in the igloo. It was already warmer inside, from the yellowish light filtering through the snow walls. I left them then, and with Eureka pacing beside me, started off in what I hoped was the direction of the beacon.

My pack weighed about ten pounds; I had food enough for three days' half-rations. I was still in reasonable shape, reasonably well-fed. With luck, I expected to make the beacon in two days' march.

I didn't have luck. I made ten miles before dark, slept cold and hungry, put in a full second day. By sundown I had covered the forty miles, but all I could see was flat plain and glare ice, all the way to the horizon. According to the chart, the beacon was built on a hundred-foot knoll that would be visible for at least twenty miles. That meant one more day, minimum.

I did the day, and another day. I rechecked my log, and edited all the figures downward; and I still should have been in sight of home base by now. That night Eureka disappeared.

The next day my legs started to go. I finished the last of my food and threw away the pack; I had a suspicion my suit heaters were about finished; I shivered all the time.

Late that day I saw Eureka, far away, crossing a slight ripple in the flat ice. Maybe he was on the trail of something to eat. I wished him luck. I had a bad fall near sunset, and had a hard time crawling into the lee of a rock to sleep.

The next day things got tough. I knew I was within a few miles of the beacon, but my suit instruments weren't good enough to pinpoint it. Any direction was as good as another. I walked east, toward the dull glare of the sun behind low clouds. When I couldn't walk anymore, I crawled. After a while I couldn't crawl anymore. I heard a buzzing from my suit pack that meant the charge was almost exhausted. It didn't seem important. I didn't hurt anymore, wasn't hungry or tired. It felt good, just floating where I was, in a warm, golden sea. Golden, the color of the Lady Raire's skin when she lay under the hot sun of Gar 28, slim and tawny. . . . Lady Raire, a prisoner, waiting for me to come for her.

I was on my feet, weaving, but upright. I picked out a rock ahead, and concentrated on reaching it. I made it and fell down and saw my own footprints there. That seemed funny. When I finished laughing, it was dark. I was cold now. I heard voices. . . .

The voices were louder, and then there was light and a man was standing over me and Eureka was sitting on his haunches beside me, washing his face.

Ommu and Ognath were all right; Lath had left the igloo and never came back; Choom was dead of gangrene. Of the four men I had sent back to the boat during the first few days, three reached it. All of the party at the boat survived. We later learned that our boat was the only one that got away from the ship. We never learned what it was we had collided with.

I was back on my feet in a day or two. The men at the beacon station were glad to have an interruption in their routine; they gave us the best of everything the station had to offer.

A couple of days later a ship arrived to take us off.

At Ahax, I went before a board of inquiry and answered a lot of questions, most of which seemed to be designed to get me to confess that it had all been my fault. But in the end they gave me a clean bill and a trip bonus for my trouble.

Assemblyman Ognath was waiting when I left the hearing room.

"I understand the board dismissed you with a modest bonus and a hint that the less you said of the disaster the better," he said.

"That's about it."

"Danger, I've always considered myself to be a man of character," he told me. "At Cyoc, I was in error. I owe you something. What are your plans?"

He gave me a sharp look when I told him. "I assume there's a story behind that—but I won't pry. . . ."

"No secret, Mister Assemblyman." I told him the story over dinner at an eating place that almost made up for thirty days on the ice. When I finished he shook his head.

"Danger, do you have any idea how long it will take you to work your passage to as distant a world as Zeridajh?"

"A long time."

"Longer than you're likely to live, at the wages you're earning."

"Maybe."

"Danger, as a politician I'm a practical

man. I have no patience with romantic quests. However, you saved my life; I have a debt to discharge. I'm in a position to offer you the captaincy of your own vessel, to undertake a mission of considerable difficulty—but one which, if you're successful, will pay you more than you could earn in twenty years below decks!"

The details were explained to me that night at a meeting in a plush suite on the top floor of a building that must have been two hundred stories high. From the terrace where I was invited to take a chair with four well-tailored and manicured gentlemen, the city lights spread out for fifty miles. Assembly-man Ognath wasn't there. One of the men did most of the talking while the other three listened.

"The task we wish you to undertake," he said in a husky whisper, "requires a man of sound judgment and intrepid character; a man without family ties or previous conflicting loyalties. I am assured you possess those qualities. The assignment also demands great determination, quick wits and high integrity. If you succeed, the rewards will be great. If you fail, you can expect a painful death, and we can do nothing to help you."

A silent-footed girl appeared with a tray of glasses. I took one and listened:

"Ahacian commercial interests have suffered badly during recent decades from the peculiarly insidious competition of a nonhuman race known as the Rish. The pattern of their activities has been such as to give rise to the conviction that more than mere mercantile ambitions are at work. We have, however, been singularly unsuccessful in our efforts to place observers among them."

"In other words, your spies haven't had any luck."

"None."

"What makes this time different?"

"You will enter Rish-controlled space openly, attended by adequate public notice. Your movements as a lone Ahacian vessel in alien-controlled space will be followed with interest by the popular screen. The Rish can hardly maintain their pretence of cordiality if they offer you open interference. Your visit to the capital, Hi-iliat, will appear no more than a casual commercial visit."

"I don't know anything about espionage," I said. "What would I do when I got there—if I got there?"

"Nothing. Your crew of four will consist of trained specialists."

"Why do you need me?"

"Precisely because you are not a specialist. Your training has been other than academic. You have faced disaster in space, and survived. Perhaps you will survive among the Rish."

It sounded simple enough: I'd be gone a year; when I got back, a small fortune would be waiting for me. The amount they mentioned made my head swim. Ognath had been wrong; it wasn't twenty years' earnings; it was forty.

"I'll take it," I said. "But I think you're wasting your money."

"We pay you nothing unless you return," the spokesman said. "In which case the outlay will not have been wasted."

The vessel they showed me in a maintenance dock at the port was a space-scarred five-thousand tonner, built twelve hundred years ago and used hard ever since. If the Rish had any agents snooping around her for hidden armor, multi-light communications gear, or superdrive auxiliaries, they didn't find them; there weren't any. Just the ancient stressed-field generators, standard navigation gear, a hold full of pre-coded computer tapes for light manufacturing operations. My crew of four were an unlikely-looking set of secret agents. Two were chinless lads with expressions of goggle-eyed innocence; one was a middle-aged man who gave the impression of having run away from a fat wife; and the last was a tall, big-handed, silent fellow with moist blue eyes.

I spent two weeks absorbing cephalotapes designed to fill in the gaps in my education. We lifted off before dawn one chilly morning, with no more fanfare than any other tramp steamer leaving harbor. I left Eureka behind with one of the tech girls from the training center. Maybe that was a clue to the confidence I had in the mission.

For the first few weeks, I enjoyed captaining my own ship, even as ancient a scow as *Jongo*. My crew stared solemnly when I suited up and painted the letters on her prow myself; to them, the idea of anthropomorphizing an artifact with a pet name was pretty weird.

We made our first planetfall without incident. I contacted the importers ashore, quoted prices, bought replacement cargo in accordance with instructions, while my four happy-go-lucky men saw the town. I didn't ask them what they'd found out; as far as I was concerned, the less I knew about their activities the better.

We went on, calling at small, unpopulous worlds, working our way deeper into the Bar, then angling toward Galactic South, swinging out into less densely populated space, where Center was a blazing arch in the screens.

We touched down on Lon, Banoon, Ostrok and twenty other worlds, as alike as small towns in the midwestern United States. And then one day we arrived at a planet which looked no different than the rest of space, but was the target we'd been feeling our way toward for five months: The Rish capital, and the place where, if I made one tiny mistake, I'd leave my bones.

The port of Hi-iliat was a booming, bustling center where great shining hulls from all the great worlds of the Bar, and even a few from Center itself, stood ranged on the miles-wide ramp system, as proud and aloof as carved Assyrian kings. We rode a rampcar in from the remote boondocks where we'd been parked by Traffic Control to a mile-wide rotunda constructed of high arched ribs of white concrete with translucent filigree-work between them. I was so busy staring up at it that I didn't see the Rish official until one of my men prodded me. I turned and was looking at a leathery five-foot oyster all ready for a walk on the beach, spindly legs and all. He was making thin buzzes and clicks that seemed to come from a locket hanging on the front side of him. It dawned on me then that it was speaking a dialect I could understand:

"All right, chaps, just in from out-system, eh? Mind stepping this way? A few formalities, won't take a skwrth."

I didn't know how long a skwrth was, but I followed him, and my four beauties followed me. He led us into a room that was like a high, narrow corridor, too brightly lit for comfort, already crowded with Men and Rish and three or four other varieties of life, none of which I had ever seen before. We sat on small stools as directed and put our hands into slots and had lights flashed in our eyes and sharp tones beeped at our ears. Whatever the test was, we must have passed, because our guide led us out into a ceilingless circular passage like a cattle run and addressed us:

"Now, chaps, as guests of the Rish Hierarchy, you're welcome to our great city and to our fair world. You'll find hostelries catering to your metabolic requirements, and if at any time you are in need of assistance, you need merely repair to the nearest sanctuary station, marked by the white pole, and you will be helped. And I must also solemnly caution you: Any act unfriendly to the Rish Hierarchy will be dealt with instantly and with the full rigor of the law. I trust you'll have a pleasant stay. Mind the step, now." He pushed a hidden control and a panel slid back and he waved us through into the concourse.

An hour later, after an ion-bath and a drink at the hotel bar, I set out to take a look at Hiliat. It was a beautiful town, full of blinding white pavement, sheer towers, tiled plazas with hundred-foot fountains, and schools and motorbikes. There were a few Men in sight, and an equal number of other aliens. The locals paid no attention to them, except to ping their bike-bells at them when they stepped out in front of them.

I found a park where orange grass as soft as velvet grew under trees with polished silver trunks and golden yellow leaves. There were odd little butterfly-like birds there, and small leathery animals the size of squirrels. Beyond it was a lake, with pretty little buildings standing up on stilts above the water; I could hear twittery music coming from somewhere. I sat on a bench and watched the big, pale sun setting across the lake. It seemed that maybe the life of a spy wasn't so bad after all.

It was twilight when I started back to the hotel. I was halfway there when four Rish on green-painted scooters surrounded me. One of them was wearing a voice box.

"Captain Billy Danger," he said in a squeak like a bat. "You are under arrest for crimes against the peace and order of the Hierarch of Rish."

CHAPTER SEVEN

The prison they took me to was a brilliantly-lit rabbit warren of partitions, blind alleys, cubicles, passages, tiny rooms where inscrutable oyster-faces stared at me while carrying on inaudible conversations that made my eardrums itch. I asked questions, but got no answers. For all I know it was the same oyster I talked to each time; it might even have been the same office. I got very hungry and thirsty and sleepy, but nobody got out any rubber hoses. I could have done worse in any small town in Mississippi.

After about an hour of these silent examinations, I wound up in a room the size of a phone booth with a Rishian wearing a talk box. He told me his name was Humekoy and that he was Chief of Physical Interrogation and Punishment. I got the impression the two duties were hard to tell apart.

"You are in a most serious position," he told me in his mechanically translated squeak. "The Rish Hierarchy has no mercy for strangers seeking to do evil. However, I am aware that you yourself have merely been used—possibly even without your knowledge—as an agency for transporting criminals. By cooperating with me fully, you may save yourself from the more unpleasant consequences of your actions. Accordingly, you will now give me full particulars of the activities of your associates."

"I want to see the Ahacian consul," I said.

"Don't waste my time," he shrilled. "What were the specific missions of the four agents who accompanied you here?"

"If my crew are under arrest, I want to see them."

"You have an imperfect grasp of the situation, Captain Danger! It is *I* who make the demands!"

"I'm afraid I can't help you."

"Nonsense, I know you Men too well. Each of you would sell his own kind to save his person."

"Then why are you afraid to let me see the consul?"

"Afraid?" He made a sound which was probably a laugh, but it lost something in translation. "Very well, then. I grant your plea."

They took me to a bigger room with softer light and left me, and a minute later an egg-bald man in dandified clothes came in, looking worried and mad.

"I understand you demanded to see me," he said and handed me a gadget and looped a similar one around his neck, with an attachment to the left ear and the Adam's apple. I followed suit.

"Look here, Danger," his voice peeped in my ear. "There's nothing I can do for you! You knew that when you came here. Insistence on seeing me serves merely to implicate Ahax."

"Who are you kidding?" I sub-vocalized. "They know all about the mission. Something leaked. That wasn't part of the deal."

"That's neither here nor there. Your duty now is to avoid any appearance that yours is an official mission."

"You think they're dumb enough to believe I'm in the spy business for myself?"

"See here, Danger, don't meddle in affairs that are beyond your grasp! You were selected for this mission because of your total illiteracy in matters of policy."

"Let's quit kidding," I said. "Why do you think they let you see me?"

"*Let* me? They practically kidnaped me!"

"Sure; this is a test. They want to see what you'll do. Species loyalty is a big thing with them—I learned that much studying tapes, back on Ahax. Every time they capture and execute a Man with no reaction from his home world, they get a little bolder."

"This is nonsense, desperate bid for rescue—"

"You made a mistake, seeing me, Mister Consul. You can't pretend you don't know me, now. Better get me out of this; if you don't, I'll spill the beans."

"What's that?" He looked shocked. "What can you tell them? You know nothing of the actual—" He cut himself off.

"I can tell them all about you, for a starter," I told him.

"Tell them what about me?"

"That you're the mastermind of the Ahacian espionage ring here on the Rish world," I said. "And everything else I can think of. Some of it might even be true."

He got his back stiffened up and gave me the ice-blue glare. "You'd play the treacher to the Ahacian Assembly, which trusted you?"

"You bureaucrats have a curious confidence in the power of one-way loyalty. You'd sell me down the river just to maintain a polite diplomatic lie; and you expect me to go, singing glad hosannas."

He struggled some more, but I had him hooked in the eye. In the end he said he'd see what he could do and went away, mopping his forehead. The oysters hustled me into an elevator and took me down into what must have been a sub-sub-basement and made me crawl through a four-foot tunnel into a dim-lit room with a strange, unpleasant smell. I was still sniffing and trying to remember what it was about the odor that made my scalp crawl when something moved in the deep gloom of the far corner and an armored, four-foot midget rose up on a set of thick legs and two over-sized eyes stared at me from the middle of its chest.

For the first five seconds I stood where I was, feeling the shock reaction slamming through my brain. Then, without any conscious decision on my part, I was diving for it. It tried to scuttle aside, but I landed on it, grabbed for what passed for its throat. Its body arced under me and the stubbly legs beat against the floor, and it broke free and went for the exit tunnel, making a sound like water gurgling down a drain. I kicked it away from the opening and it curled up and rolled to a neutral corner and I stood over it, breathing hard and looking for a soft spot to attack.

"Peace!" the word sounded grotesque coming from what looked like an oversized armadillo. "I yield, Master! Have mercy on poor Srat!" Then it made sounds that were exactly like an Australian bush baby—or a crying child.

"That's right," I said, and my voice had a

high, quavering note. I could feel the goose-
flesh on my arms, just from being this close to
the thing. "I'm not ready to kill you yet. First
you're going to tell me things!"

"Yes, Master! Poor Srat will tell Master
everything he knows! All, all!"

"There was a ship—wasp-waisted, copper-
colored, big. It answered our distress call.
Bugs like you came out of it. They shot me up,
but I guess they didn't know much human
anatomy. And they took the Lady Raire.
Where did they take her? Where is she? What
did they do to her?"

"Master, let poor Srat think!" he gurgled,
and I realized I'd been kicking it with every
question mark.

"Don't think—just give me the answers." I
drew a deep breath and felt the rage draining
away and my hands started to shake from the
reaction.

"Master, poor Srat doesn't understand
about the lady—" It *oof*'ed in anticipation
when I took a step toward it.

"The ship, yes," it babbled. "Long ago poor
Srat remembers such a ship, all in the beauty
of its mighty form, like a great mother. But
that was long, long ago!"

"Three years," I said. "On a world out in the
Arm."

"No, Master! Forty years have passed away
since last poor Srat glimpsed the great
mother-shape! And that was deep in Fringe
Space—" It stopped suddenly, as if it had said

too much, and I kicked it again.

"Poor Srat is in exile," it shined. "So far, so far from the heaving, oil-black bosom of the deeps of H'eeaq."

"Is that where they took her? To H'eeaq?"

It groaned. "Weep for great H'eeaq, Master. Weep for poor Srat's memories of that which was once, and can never be again. . . ."

I listened to the blubbering and groaning, and piece by piece, got the story from it: H'eeaq, a lone world, a hundred lights out toward Galactic Zenith, where Center spread over the sky like a blazing roof; the discovery that the sun was on the verge of a nova explosion; the flight into space, the years—centuries—of gypsy wandering. And a landing on a Rish-controlled world, a small brush with the Rish law—and forty years of slavery. By the time it was finished, I was sitting on the bench by the wall, feeling cold, washed out of all emotion, for the first time in three years. Kicking this poor waif wouldn't bring the Lady Raire back home. That left me with nothing at all.

"And Master" poor Srat whimpered. "Has Master, too, aroused the cruel ire of these Others?"

"Yeah, I guess you could say that. They're using me for a test case—" I cut myself off. I wasn't ready to start gossiping with the thing.

"Master—poor Srat can tell Master many things about these Rishs. Things that will help him."

"It's a little late for that," I said. "I've already had my say. Humekoy wasn't impressed."

The H'eeaq crept closer to me. "No, Master, listen to poor Srat: Of mercy, the Rish-things know nothing. But in matters of business ethic. . . ."

I was asleep when they came for me. Four guards with symbols painted on their backs herded me along to a circular room where a lone Rish who might have been Humekoy sat behind a desk under a spotlight. Other Rish came in, took seats along the walls behind me. My buddy, the Ahacian consul, was nowhere in sight.

"What will you offer for your freedom?" the presiding Rish asked bluntly.

I stood there remembering what poor Srat had told me about the Rish and wondering whether to believe him.

"Nothing," I said.

"You offer nothing for your life?"

"It's already mine. If you kill me you'll be stealing."

"And if we imprison you?"

"Stealing is stealing. My life is mine, not yours."

I felt the silent buzzing that meant they

were talking it over. Then Humekoy picked up two rods, a white one and a red one, from the desk. He held the white one out to me.

"You will depart the Rish world at once," he said. "Take this symbol of Rish magnanimity and go."

I shook my head, and felt the sweat start up. "I'll take my life and freedom because it's mine, not as a gift. I don't want *any* gifts from you; no gifts at all."

"You refuse the mercy of the Hierarch?" Humekoy's canned voice went up off the scale.

"All I want is what's mine."

More silent conversation. Humekoy put the rods back on the desk.

"Then go, Captain Danger. You have your freedom."

"What about my crew?"

"They are guilty. They will pay their debt."

"They're no good to you. I suppose you've already pumped them dry. Why not let them go?"

"Ah, you crave a gift after all?"

"No. I'll pay for them."

"So? What payment do you offer?"

Poor Srat had briefed me on this, too. I knew what I had to do, but my mouth felt dry and my stomach was quivering. We bargained for ten minutes before we agreed on a price.

My right eye.

They were skillful surgeons. They took the eye out without anesthetic, other than a stiff drink of what tasted like refrigerant fluid. Humekoy stood by and watched with every indication of deep interest. As for me, I had already learned about pain: the body is capable of registering only a certain amount of it; about what you'd get from laying your palm on a hot plate. After that, it's all the same. I yelled and screamed a little, and kicked around a bit, but it was over very quickly. They packed the empty socket with something cold and wet that numbed it in a few seconds. In half an hour I was back on my feet, feeling dizzy and with a sort of gauzy veil between my remaining eye and the world.

They took me to the port and my crew were there ahead of me, handcuffed and looking pale green around the ears. And the consul was there, too, with his hands clamped up as tight as the rest.

"It has been a fair exchange, Captain Danger," Humekoy told me after the others were aboard. "These paid cheats have garnered their petty harvest of data on industrial and port facilities, volume of shipping and sophistication of equipment, on which to base estimates of Rish assault capability. And in return, the Hierarch has gained valuable information for proper assessment of you humans. Had we acted on the basis of impressions gained by study of the persons so cleverly trained to delude us heretofore, we might have made a serious blunder."

We parted on that note, not as pals, exactly, but with what might be described as a mutual wary respect. At the last minute a rampcar pulled up and a pair of Rish guards dumped poor Srat out.

"The creature aided, indirectly, in our rapprochement," Humekoy said. "His payment is his freedom. Perhaps you, too, may have an account to settle."

"Put him aboard," I said. "He and I will have a lot of things to talk over before I get back to Ahax."

By the time the fifty-seven-day voyage was over, I knew as much about H'eeaq as poor Srat could tell me.

"Why these mistaken kin of mine may have stolen a lady of Master's kind, I can't say," he insisted. But as to where—he had a few ideas on that.

"There are worlds, Master, where long ago H'eeaq established markets for the complex molecules so abundantly available to her in those days. Our vessels call there still, and out of regard for past ties perhaps, the indwellers supply our needs for stores. And in return, we give them what we can."

He gave me the details of a few of these old

marketplaces—worlds far out in Fringe Space, where few questions were asked, and a human was a rare freak.

"We'll go take a look," I said. "As soon as I collect my pay."

At Ahax, Traffic Control allotted me a slot at the remotest corner of the port. We docked and my four cheery crewmen were gone in a rampcar before I finished securing the command deck. I told Srat to follow me, and started off to walk the two miles to the nearest power way. I rampcar went past in a hurry in the next lane over, headed out toward where my tub was parked. I thought about hailing it, but even with the chill wind blowing, walking felt good after the weeks in space.

Inside the long terminal building, a P.A. voice was droning something. Srat made a gobbling noise and said, "Master, they speak of you!" I looked where he pointed with one flipper and saw my face looking down from a public screen.

". . . distinguishing scar on the right side of the neck and jaw," the voice was saying. "It is the duty of any person seeing this man to detain him and notify Central Authority at once!"

Nobody seemed to be looking my way. I was wearing a plain gray shipsuit and a light windbreaker with the collar turned up far enough to cover the scar; I didn't look much different than a lot of other space-burned crew types. Poor Srat was crouching and quivering; they hadn't put him on the air, but he would attract attention with his whimpering. We had to get to cover, fast. I turned and headed for the nearest ramp exit and as I reached the vestibule a woman's voice called my name. I spun and saw a familiar face; Nacy, the little tech operator I'd left Eureka with.

"I was in Ops Three when your clearance request came, four hours ago," she said in a fast whisper. She saw the patch over my eye and her voice faltered and went on: "I thought . . . after all, no one expected you to come back . . . it would be nice to come down and meet you. Then . . . I heard the announcement. . . ."

"What's it all about, Nacy?"

She shook her head. She was a pert little girl with a turned-up nose and very white, even teeth. "I don't know, Billy. Someone said you'd gone against your orders, turned back early—"

"Yeah. There's something in that. But you don't want to be seen talking to me—"

"Billy—maybe if you went to them voluntarily . . ."

"I have a funny feeling near the back of my

neck that says that would be a wrong play."

Her face looked tight; she nodded. "I think I understand." She took a bite of her lip. "Come with me." She turned and started across the lobby. Srat plucked at my sleeve.

"You'll do better on your own," I said, and followed her.

She led me through a door marked for private use, along a plain corridor with lots of doors, out through a small personnel entry onto a parking lot full of ramp vehicles.

"Good thinking, girl," I said. "You'd better fade out fast now—"

"Just a minute." She ducked back inside. I went to a small mail-carrier, found the controls unlocked. I started it up and backed it around by the door as it swung open and a sleek pepper and salt and tan animal stalked through, looking relaxed, as always.

"Eureka!" I called, and the old boy stopped and looked my way, then reached the car in one bound and was in beside me. I looked up and Nacy was watching from the door.

"Thanks for everything," I said. "I don't know why you took the chance, but thanks."

"Maybe it's because you're what's known as a romantic figure," she said and whirled and was gone before I could ask her what that meant.

I pulled the car out and into a lane across the ramp, keeping it at an easy speed. There was a small click from over my head and a voice said, "Seven-eight-nine-o, where do you think you're going?"

"Fuel check," I mumbled.

"Little late, aren't you? You heard the clear ramp order."

"Yeah, what's it all about?"

"Pickup order out on some smuggler that gave Control the slip a few minutes ago. Now get off the ramp!" He clicked off. I angled right as if I were headed for the maintenance bay at the end of the line, but at the last second I veered left and headed out toward where I'd parked *Jongo*. I could see rampcars buzzing back and forth, off to my left; I passed two uniformed men, on foot. One of them stared at me and I kept my chin down in my collar and waved to him. A hundred yards from the tub, I saw the cordon of cars around it. So much for my chances of a slick takeoff under their noses. I pulled the car offside between a massive freighter that looked as if it hadn't been moved for a couple of hundred years, and a racy yacht that reminded me of Lord Desroy's, and tried to make my brain think. It didn't seem to want to. My eyes kept wandering back to the fancy enamel-inlaid trim around the entry lock of the yacht. The port was open and I could see the gleam of hand-rubbed finishes inside. . . .

I was out of the car and across to the yacht before I realized I'd made a decision. Eureka went in ahead of me, as if he owned the boat. Just as I got a foot on the carpeted four-step ladder, one of the pedestrian cops came into sight around the side of the old freighter. He saw me and broke into a run, fumbling with a holster at his side in a way that said he had orders to shoot. I unfroze and started up, knowing I wouldn't make it, and heard a scuffling sound and a heavy thud and a crash of fire that cracked and scorched the inlay by the door. I looked back and he was spread out on the pavement, out cold, and poor Srat was untangling himself from his legs. He scrambled in behind me and I tripped the port-secure lever and ran for the flight deck. I slammed the main drive lever to full emergency lift-off position and felt my back teeth shake as the yacht screamed off the ramp, splitting the atmosphere of Ahax like a meterorite outward-bound.

The ship handled like a yachtsman's dream; for the first few hours I ducked and bobbed in an evasion pattern that took us out through the planetary patrols. I kept the comm channels open and listened to a lot of excited talk that told me I'd picked the personal transportation of an Ahacian official whose title translated roughly as Assistant Dictator. After a while Assemblyman Ognath came on, looking very red around the ears, and showed me a big smile as phoney as a UN peace proposal.

"Captain Danger, there's been a misunderstanding," he warbled. "The police officers you may have seen at the port were merely a guard of honor—"

"Somebody forgot to tell the gun-handlers about that," I said in a breezy tone that I thought would have the maximum irritant value. "I had an idea maybe you fellows decided forty years' pay was too much to spend, after all. But that's OK; I'll accept this bucket as payment in full."

"Look here, Danger," Ognath let the paper smile drop. "Bring the vessel back, and I'll employ my influence to see that you're dealt with leniently."

"Thanks; I've had a sample of your influence. I don't think I'd live through another."

"You're a fool! Every civilized world within ten parsecs will be alerted; you'll be hunted down and blasted without mercy—unless you turn back now!"

"I guess the previous owner is after somebody's scalp, eh, Ognath? Too bad."

I gave him, and a couple of naval types who followed him, some more funny answers and in the process managed to get a fair idea of the interference I could expect to run into. I had to dodge three patrols in the first twenty hours; by the thirtieth hour I was running directly toward Galactic Zenith with nothing ahead but the Big Black.

"Give me the coordinates of the nearest of the worlds where you H'eeaq used to trade," I ordered Srat.

"It is distant, Master. So far away, so lonely. The world called Drope."

"We'll try it anyway." I said. "Maybe somewhere out there we'll run into a little luck."

The yacht was fueled and supplied in a way that suggested that someone had been prepared for any sudden changes in the political climate back home. It carried food, wines, a library that was all the most self-indulgent dictator could want to while away those long, dull days in space.

I showed Srat how to handle the controls so that he could relieve me whenever I felt like taking a long nap or sampling the library. I asked him why he had stuck with me, but he just looked at me with those goggle-eyes, and for the first time in many weeks it struck me what a strange-looking thing he was. You can get used to anything, even a H'eeaq.

Eureka was better company than the alien, in spite of not being able to talk. He settled in in a cabin full of frills that conjured up pictures of a dance-hall floozie with the brains of a Pekinese and a voice to match. Fortunately, the dictator's taste in music and books was closer to mine than his choice of mistresses. There were tapes aboard on everything from ancient human history to the latest techniques in cell-surgery, thoroughly indexed. I sampled them all.

The Fringe worlds, I learned, were the Museum of the Galaxy. These lonely planets had once, long eons ago, been members of the tightly packed community of Center; their races had been the first in the young Galaxy to explore out through the Bar and Eastern Arm, where their remote descendants still thrived. Now the ancient Mother-worlds lingered on, living out the twilight of their long careers, circling dying suns, far out in the cool emptiness of the space between Galaxies. One of those old races, Srat assured me, was the ancestral form of Man—not that I'd recognize the relationship if I encountered a representative of the tribe.

One day I ran through a gazeteer of the Western Arm, found a listing of an obscure sun I was pretty sure was Sol and coded its reference into the index. The documentary that came onto the view-screen showed me dull-steel ball bearing with a brilliant high-light that the voice track said was the system's tenth planet. Number nine looked about the same, only bigger. Eight and seven were big fuzz-balls flattened at the poles. I had just about decided I had the wrong star when Saturn swam into view. The sight of that old familiar ring made me feel homesick, as if I'd spent the long happy hours of childhood there. I recognized Big Jupe too. The camera came in close on this one, and then there were surface scenes on the moons. They looked just like Luna.

Mars was a little different than the pictures

I remembered seeing; the ice caps were bigger, and in the close scan the camera moved in on what looked like the ruins of a camp not a city, just a lash-up collection of metal huts and fallen antennas, such as a South Pole expedition might have left behind. And then I was looking at Earth, swimming there on the screen, cool and misty green and upside down, with Europe at the bottom and Africa at the top. I stared at it for half a minute before I noticed that the ice caps were wrong. The northern one covered most of Germany and the British Isles, and as the camera swung past, I could see that it spread down across North America as far as Kansas. And there wasn't any south polar cap. Antarctica was a crescent-shaped island, all by itself in the ocean, ice-free; and Australia was connected to Indochina. I knew then the pictures had been made a long time ago.

The camera moved in close, and I saw oceans and jungles, deserts and ice-fields, but nowhere any sign of Man. The apparent altitude at the closest approach was at least ten thousand feet, but even from that height I could make out herds of game. But whether they were mammoths and megatheria or something even older, I couldn't tell.

Then the scene shifted to Venus, which looked like Neptune, only smaller and brighter, and I switched the viewer off and made myself a long, strong drink and settled down for the long run ahead.

CHAPTER EIGHT

Drope was a lone world, circling a tired old star the color of sunset in Nevada. No hostile interceptors rose to meet me, but there was no welcoming committee either. We grounded at what Srat said was a port, but all I saw was a windblown wasteland with a few hillocks around it, under a purplish-black sky without a star in sight, Center being below the horizon. The air was cold, and the wind seemed to be whispering sad stories in the dusk. I went back aboard; I dined well and drank a bottle of old Ahacian wine and listened to music, but it seemed to be telling sad stories, too. Just before dawn Srat came back with a report that a H'eeaq ship had called—about a century ago, Earth time.

"That doesn't help us much," I pointed out.

"At least," Poor Srat got down and wriggled in the dust, but I sensed a certain insolence in his voice—"at least Master knows now I speak truly of the voyages of the H'eeaq."

"Either that or you're a consistent liar," I said, and stopped. My tone of voice when I talked to the midget reminded me of something, but I couldn't say what it was.

Srat's informant had mentioned the name of the H'eeaq vessel's next port of call: A world known as E'el, ten lights farther out into intergalactic space, which meant a two weeks' run. I set ship time up on a cycle as close to Earth time as I could estimate, and for a while I tried to sleep eight hours at a stretch, eat three meals a day, and maintain some pretense of night and day; but the habit of nearly six years in space was too strong. I soon reverted to three on, three off, with meals every other off-period.

We picked up E'el on our screens at last, a small, dim star not even shown on the standard charts. I set the yacht down on a grassy plain near a town made of little mud-colored domes and went into the village with Srat. There was nothing there but dust and heat and a few shy natives who scuttled inside their huts as we passed. An hour of that was enough.

After that we called at a world that Srat called Zlinn, where a swarm of little atmosphere fliers about as sturdy as Spads came up and buzzed us like irate hornets. They refused

us permission to disembark. If any H'eeaq
vessel had been there in the last few decades,
it was their secret.

We visited Lii, a swamp-world where vast
batteries of floodlights burned all day under a
dying sun, and Shoramnath, where everyone
had died since Srat's last visit, and we walked
around among the bones and the rusted
machines and the fallen-in buildings, and
wondered what had hit them; and we saw Far,
and Z'reeth, and on Kish they let us land and
then attacked us, just a few seconds pre-
maturely, so that we made it back to the lock
and lifted off in the middle of a barrage of HE
fire that burned some of the shine off the hull.
Suicide fliers threw themselves at us as we
streaked for space; they must have been tough
organisms, because some of them survived
the collisions and clung to the hull and I heard
them yammering and rat-tat-tatting there for
minutes after we had left the last of the atmosphere behind.

On Tith, there were fallen towers that had
once been two miles high, lying in rows pointing north, like a forest felled by a meteor
strike. We talked to the descendants of the
tower builders, and they told me that a H'eeaq
ship had called; a year ago, a century ago, a
thousand years—it was all the same to them.

We pushed on, hearing rumors, legends,
hints that a vessel like the one I described had
been seen once, long ago, or had visited the
next world out-system, or that creatures like

Srat had been found, dead, on an abandoned moon. Then even the rumors ran out; and Srat was fresh out of worlds.

"The trail's cold," I told him. "There's nothing out here but death and decay and legends. I'm turning back for Center."

"Only a little farther, Master," Poor Srat pleaded. "Master will find what he seeks, if only he pressed on." He didn't have quite the whimpering tone now that he used to use. I wondered about Poor Srat; what he had up his sleeve.

"One more try," I said. "Then I turn back and try for Center, even if every post office this side of Earth has my picture in it."

But the next sun that swam into range was one of a small cluster; eight small, long-lived suns, well past Sol on the evolutionary scale, but still in their prime. Srat almost tied himself into a knot.

"Well do I remember the Eight Suns, Master! These are rich worlds, and generous. After we filled our holds here with succulent lichens—"

"I don't want any succulent lichens," I cut off his rhapsody. "All I want is a hot line on a H'eeaq ship."

I picked the nearest of the suns, swung in on a navigation beam from Drath, the ninth planet, with Srat doing the talking to Control, and sat the ship down on a ramp that looked as though it had survived some heavy bombardments in its day. A driverless flatcar riding on an airstream came out to pick us up. We rode in it toward a big pinkish-gray structure across the field. Beyond it, a walled city sprawled up across a range of rounded hills. The sky was a pre-storm black, but the sun's heat baked down through the haze like a smelter.

There were rank, tropical trees and fleshy-looking flowers growing along the drive that ran the final hundred yards. Up close, I could see cracks in the building.

There were no immigration formalities to clear through, just a swarm of heavy-bodied, robed humanoids with skin like hard olive-green plastic and oversized faces—if you can call something that looks like a tangle of fish guts a face. Eureka stayed close to my side, rubbing against my leg as we pushed through the crowd inside the big arrival shed. Srat followed, making the *off*!ing sounds that meant he didn't like it here. I told him to find someone he could talk to, and try for some information; he picked a non-Drathian, a frail little knob-kneed creature creeping along by a wall with the fringe of its dark blue cloak dragging in the mud. It directed him along to a stall at the far side of the lobby, which turned out to be a sort of combination labor exchange and lost-and-found. A three-hundred-pound Drathian in dirty saffron toga listened to Srat, then rumbled an answer.

"No vessel of H'eeaq has called here, says he, Master" Srat reported. "Drath trades with no world; the produce of Drath is the most magnificent in the Universe; he demands why anyone would seek items made elsewhere. He says also that he can offer an attractive price on a thousand tons of glath."

"What's glath?"

"Mud, Master," he translated.

"Tell him thanks, but I've sworn off." We left him and pushed on through to take a look at the town.

The buildings were high, blank-fronted, stuccoed in drab shades of ochre and pink and mauve. There was an eerie feeling hanging over the place, as if everyone was away, attending a funeral. The click and clatter and pat-pat of our assorted styles of feet were jarringly loud. A hot rain started up, to add to the cheer. It struck me again how alike cities were, on worlds all across the Galaxy. Where creatures gather together to build dwellings the system of arranging them in rows along open streets is almost universal. This one was like a Mexican village, with water; all poverty and mud. I saw nothing that would pass for a policeman, an information office, a city hall or government house. After an hour of walking I was wet to the skin, cold to the bone, and depressed to the soul.

I was ready to give it up and head back to the ship when the street widened out into a plaza crowded with stalls and carts under tattered awnings of various shades of gray. Compared to the empty streets, the place looked almost gay.

The nearest stall displayed an assortment of dull-colored balls, ranging from lemon to grapefruit size. Srat tried to find out what they were, but the answer was untranslatable. Another bin was filled with what seemed to be dead beetles. I gathered they were edible, if you liked that sort of thing. The next displayed baubles and gimcracks made of polished metal and stone, like jewelry in every time and clime. Most of the metal was dull yellow, lead-heavy gold, and I felt a faint stir of an impulse to fill my pockets. Up ahead, an enterprising merchant had draped the front of his stall with scraps of cloth. From the colors, I judged he was colorblind, at least in what I thought of as the visible spectrum. One piece of rag caught my eye; it was a soft, silvery gray. I fingered it and felt a shock go through me as if I'd grabbed a hot wire. But it wasn't electricity that made my muscles go rigid; it was the unmistakable feel of Zeridajhan cloth.

It was a piece about two feet long and a foot wide, raggedly cut. It might have been the back panel from a shipsuit. I started to lift it and the stall-keeper grabbed for it, and cracked something in the local language, a sound like hot fat sizzling. I didn't let go.

"Tell him I want to buy it," I told Srat.

The stall-keeper tugged and made more hot-fat sounds.

"Master, he doesn't understand the trade tongue," Srat said.

The merchant was getting excited, now. He

made an angry buzzing and yanked hard; I ripped the cloth out of his balled fists; then Srat was clutching at my arm and saying, "Beware, Master!"

I looked around. A large Drathian who could have been the same one who offered me the load of glath except for the white serape across his chitinous shoulder was pushing through the gathering crowd toward me. Something about him didn't look friendly. As he came up, he crackled at the merchant. The merchant crackled back. The big Drathian planted himself in front of me and spit words at me.

"Master," Srat gobbled, "the Rule-keeper demands to know why you seek to rob the merchant!"

"Tell him I'll pay well for the cloth." I took out a green trade chip that was worth six months' pay back on the Bar Worlds, and handed it over, but the Rule-keeper still didn't seem satisfied.

"Find out where he got the cloth, Srat," I said. There was more talk then; I couldn't tell whether the big Drathian was a policeman, a guild official, a racket boss, or an ambulance-chasing shyster, but he seemed to pull a lot of weight. The stall-keeper was scared to death of him.

"Master, the merchant swears he came by the rag honestly; yet if Master insists, he will make him a gift of it."

"I'm not accusing him of anything. I just want to know where the cloth came from."

This time the bully-boy did the talking, ended by pointing across the plaza.

"Master, a slave sold the cloth to the merchant."

"What kind of slave?"

"Master . . . a Man-slave."

"Like me?"

"He says—yes, Master."

I let my elbow touch the butt of my filament pistol. If the crowd that had gathered around to watch and listen decided to turn nasty, it wouldn't help much; but it was comforting anyway.

"Where did he see this Man-slave?"

"Here, Master; the slave is the property of the Least Triarch."

"Find out where the Triarch lives."

"There, Master." Srat pointed to a dusty blue facade rising behind the other buildings like a distant cliff-face. "That is the palace of His Least Greatness."

"Let's go." I started past the Rule-keeper and he jabbered at Srat.

"Master, he says you have forgotten his bribe."

"My mistake." I handed over another chip. "Tell him I'd like his assistance in getting an interview with the Triarch."

A price was agreed on and he led the way

across the plaza and through the network of
dark streets, along a complicated route that
ended in a tiled courtyard with a yellow glass
roof that made it look almost like a sunny day.
There were trees and flowering shrubs
around like a sunny day. There were trees and
flowering shrubs around a reflecting pool, a
shady cloister along the far side. Srat was nervous; he perched on a chair and mewed to
himself. Eureka stretched out and stared
across at a tall blue-legged bird wading in the
pool.

A small Drathian came over and took
orders. He asked Eureka three times what
he'd have; he couldn't seem to get the idea
that the old cat didn't speak the language. The
drinks he brought were a thick, blue syrup
with a taste of sulfur and honey. Srat sniffed
his cup and said, "Master must not drink
this," and proceeded to swallow his share in
one gulp. I stared into the shadows under the
arcade where my guide had disappeared, and
pretended to nibble the drink. Rain drummed
on the glass overhead. It was steamy hot, like
a greenhouse. After half an hour, the Drathian
came back, with a friend.

The newcomer was six feet tall, five feet
wide, draped in dark blue velvet and hung
with ribbons and tassels and fringes like a
Victorian bonnet. He was introduced as
Hruba. He was the Triarch's majordomo, and
he spoke very bad, but understandable lingua.

"You may crave one boon of His Greatness," he stated. In return, he will accept a gift."

"I understand the Triarch owns a human slave," I said. "I'd like to see him, if His Greatness has no objection."

The majordomo agreed, and gave orders to a servant; in ten minutes the servant was back, prodding a man along ahead of him.

He was a stocky, strong-looking fellow with close-cropped black hair, well-cut features, dressed in a plain dark blue kilt. There was an ugly, two-inch scar on his left side, just below the ribs. He saw me and stopped dead and his face worked.

"You're a human being!" he gasped—in Zeridajhi.

His name was Huvile, and he had been a prisoner for ten years. He'd been captured, he said, when his personal boat had developed drive control troubles and had carried him off course into Fringe Space.

"In the name of humanity, Milord," he begged, "buy my freedom." He looked as if he wanted to kneel, but the big Drathian servant was holding his arm in a two-handed grip.

"I'll do what I can," I said.

"Save me, Milord—and you'll never regret it! My family is wealthy—" That was as far as he got before Hruba waved an arm and the servant hustled him away.

I looked at the majordomo.

"How much?"

"He is yours."

I expressed gratification, and offered money in return. Hruba indicated that Bar money was hard to spend on Drath. I ran through a list of items from *Jongo II*'s well-stocked larders and storage hold; we finally agreed on a mixed consignment of drugs, wines, clothing and sense-tapes.

"His Greatness will be gratified," Hruba said expansively, "at this opportity to display his graciousness." He aimed a sense-organ at me. "Ah . . . you wouldn't by chance wish to accept a second slave?"

"Another Man?"

"As it happens."

"How many more humans have you got?"

"His Greatness owns many properties; but only the two humans." His voice got almost confidential: "Useful, of course, but a trifle, ah, intractable. But *you*'ll have no trouble on that score, I'm sure."

We dickered for ten minutes and settled on a deal that would leave *Jongo II*'s larder practically stripped. It was lucky the Triarch didn't own three men; I couldn't have afforded any more.

"I will send porters and a car to fetch these tifles from your vessel," Hruba said, "which

His Greatness accepts out of sentiment. You wish the slaves delivered there?"

"Never mind; I'll take them myself." I started to get up.

Hruba made a shocked noise. "You would omit the ceremonies of Agreement, of Honorable Dealing, of Mutual Satisfaction?"

I calmed him down and he sent his staff scurrying for the necessary celebratory paraphernalia.

"Srat, you go to the ship, hand over the goods we agreed on, and see that the men get aboard all right. Take Eureka with you."

"Master, Poor Srat is afraid to go alone—and he fears for Master—"

"Better get going or they'll be there ahead of you."

He made a sad sound and hurried away.

"Your other slave," the majordomo pointed. Across the court, a Drathian servant came out from a side entry leading a slim figure in a gray kilt like Huvile had worn.

"You said another man," I said stupidly.

"Eh? You doubt it is a Man?" he asked in a stiff voice. "It is not often that the probity of His Least Greatness is impugned in his own Place of Harmonious Accord!"

"My apologies," I tried to recover. "It was just a matter of terminology. I didn't expect to see a female."

"Very well, a female Man—but still a Man and a sturdy worker," the majordomo came back. "Not so large as the other, perhaps, but diligent, diligent. Still, His Greatness would not have you feel cheated. . . ." His voice faded off. He was watching me as I watched the servant leading the girl past, some twenty feet away. She had a scar on her side, exactly like Huvile's. Beside the horny, gray-green throax of the Drathian beside her, her human breast looked incredibly vulnerable. Then she turned her head my way and I saw that it was the Lady Raire.

For a long, echoing instant, time stood still. Then she was past. She hadn't seen me, sitting on the deep shade of the canopy. I heard myself make some kind of sound and realized I had half risen from my chair.

"This slave is of some particular interest for you?" the majordomo inquired, and I could tell from the edge on his voice that his commercial instinct was telling him he had missed a bet somewhere.

I sat down. "No," I managed to croak. "I was wondering . . . about the scars. . . ."

"Have no fear; the cicatrice merely marks the point where the control drive is embedded. However, perhaps I should withdraw His Greatness's offer of this gift, since it is less than you expected, lest the generosity of the Triarch suffer reflection. . . ."

"My mistake," I said. "I'm perfectly satisfied." I could feel my heart slamming inside my chest. I felt as though the universe was balanced on a knife-edge. One wrong word from me and the whole fragile deal would collapse.

The liquor pots arrived then, and conversation was suspended while my host made a big thing of tasting half a dozen varieties of syrupy booze and organizing the arrangement of outsize drinking pots on the table. I sat tight and sweated bullets and wondered how it was going back at the ship.

The Drathian offered the local equivalent of a toast. While my host sucked his cup dry, I pretended to take a sip, but he noticed and writhed his face at me.

"You do not sup! Is your zeal for Honorable Dealing less than complete?"

This time I had to drink. The stuff had a sweet overflavor, but left an aftertaste of iron filings. I forced it down. After that, there was another toast. He watched to be sure I drank it. I tried not to think about what the stuff was doing to my stomach. I fixed my thoughts on a face I had just seen, looking no older than the day I had seen it last, nearly four years before; and the smooth, suntanned skin, and the hideous scar that marred it.

There was a lot of chanting and exchanging

of cups, and I chewed another drink. Srat
would be showing Milady Raire to a cabin
now, and she'd be feeling the softness of a
human-style bed, a rug under her feet, the
tingle of the ion-bath for the first time in four
years. . . .

"Another toast!" Hruba called. His
command of lingua was slipping; the booze
was having a powerful effect on him. It was
working on me, too. My head was buzzing and
there was a frying-egg feeling in my stomach.
My arm felt almost too heavy to lift. The taste
of the liquor was cloying in my mouth. When
the next cup was passed my way I pushed it
aside.

"I've had all I can take," I said, and felt my
tongue slur the words. It was hard to push the
chair back and stand. Hruba rose, too. He was
swaying slightly—or maybe it was just my
vision.

"I confess surprise, Man," he said. "Your
zeal in the pledging of honor exceeded even
my own. My brain swims in a sea of conse-
crated wine!" He turned to a servant standing
by and accepted a small box from him.

"The control device governing your new ac-
quisition," he said and handed the box over to
me. I took it and my finger touched a hidden
latch and the lid valved open. There was a
small plastic ovoid inside, bedded in floss.

"Wha's . . . what's this?"

"Ah, you are unfamiliar with our Drathian

devices!" He plucked the egg from its niche and waved it under my nose.

"This gnurled wheel; on the first setting, it administers sharp reminder; at the second position . . ." he pushed the control until it clicked, ". . . an attack of angina which doubles the object in torment. And at the third . . . but I must not demonstrate the third setting, eh? Or you will find yourself with a dead slave on your hands, his heart burned to charcoal by a magnesium element buried in the organ itself!" He tossed the control back into the box and sat down heavily. "That pertaining to the female is in the possession of her tender; he will leave it in the hands of your servant. You'll have no trouble with 'em. . . ." He made a sound that resembled a hiccup. "Best return to zero setting the one I handled; if its subject lacks stamina, he may be dead by now."

I tilted the box and dumped the ovoid on the ground and stamped on it; it crunched like a blown egg. Hruba came out of his chair in a rush. "Here—what are you doing!" He stared down at the smashed controller, then at me. "Have you lost your mind, Man?"

"I'm going now," I said, and went past him toward the passage I had entered by, a long time ago, it seemed. Behind me, Hruba was shouting in the local dialect. A servant jittered in front of me, and I yanked my pistol out and waved it and he jumped aside.

Out in the street, night had fallen, and the
wet pavement glimmered under the yellow-
green glare of lanterns set on the building
fronts. I felt deathly ill. The street seemed to
be rising up under my feet. I staggered, stayed
on my feet by holding onto the wall. A pain
like a knife-thrust stabbed into my stomach. I
headed off in the direction of the port, made
half a block before I had to lean against the
wall and retch. When I straightened there
were half a dozen Drathians standing by,
watching me with their obscene faces. I yelled
something at them, and they scattered back,
and I went on.

I passed the plaza where I had found the
Zeridajhi cloth, recognized the street along
which Srat and Eureka and I had come. It
seemed to be a steep hill, now. My legs felt
like soft tallow. I fell and got up and fell again.
I retched until my stomach was a dry knot of
pain. It was harder getting to my feet this
time. My lungs were on fire. The pain in my
head was like a hammer swinging against my
temples. My eyes were crossing, and I stumbled along between twinned walls, seeing the
two-headed Drathians retreat before me.

Then I saw the port ahead, the translucent,
glowing dome rising at the end of the narrow
alleyway. Not much farther, now. Srat would
be wondering what happened; maybe he
would be waiting, just ahead. And at the ship,
the Lady Raire. . . .

I was lying on my face, and the sky was

spinning slowly over me, a pitch-black canopy with the great dim blur of Center sprawled across it, and the faint avenue that was the Bar reaching out to trail off into the dwindling spiral curve of the Eastern Arm. I found the pavement under me, and pushed against it, and got to my knees, then to my feet. I could see the ship across the ramp, tall and rakish, her high polish dimmed by the years of hard use, her station lights glaring amber from high on her slim prow. I steadied myself and started across toward her, and as I did the rectangle of light that was the open port narrowed and winked out. The amber lights flicked out and the red and green pattern of her running lights sprang up. I stopped dead and felt a drumming start up, vibrating through the pavement under my feet.

I started to run then, and my legs were broken straws that collapsed and my head hit and the blow cleared it for a moment. I got my chin up off the pavement; and *Jongo II* lifted, standing up away from the surface on a tenuous pillar of blue flame that lengthened as she rose. Then she was climbing swiftly into the night, tilting away, dwindling above the licking tongue of pale fire that shrank, became a tiny point of twinkling yellow, and was gone.

They were all around me in a tight circle. I stared at their horny shins, their sandaled feet, as alien as an alligator's, and felt the icy sweat clammy on my face. Deathly sickness rose inside me in a wave that knotted my stomach and left me quivering like a beached jellyfish.

The legs around me stirred and gave way to a tall Drathian in the white serape of a Rule-keeper. Hard hands clamped on me, dragged me to my feet. A light glared in my face.

"Man, the Rule-keeper demands you produce the two slaves given as a gift to you by His Least Greatness!"

"Gone," I gargled the words. "Trusted Srat. Filthy midget. . . ."

"Man, you are guilty of a crime of the first category! Illegal manumission of slaves! To redress these crimes, the Rule-keeper demands a fine of twice the value of the slaves, plus triple bribes for himself and his attendants!"

"You're out of luck," I said. "No money . . . no ship . . . all gone. . . ."

I felt myself blacking out then. I was dimly aware of being carried, of lights glaring on me, later of a pain that seemed to tear me open, like a rotten fruit; but it was all remote, far away, happening to someone else. . . .

I came to myself lying on a hard pallet on a stone floor, still sick, but clear-headed now. For a while, I looked at the lone glare-bulb in the ceiling and tried to remember what had happened, but it was all a confused fog. I sat up and a red-hot hook grabbed at my side. I pulled back the short, coarse-weave jacket I was wearing, and saw a livid, six-inch cut under my ribs, neatly stitched with tough thread. It was the kind of wound that would heal in a few weeks and leave a welted scar; a scar like I'd seen recently, in the sides of Huvile and the Lady Raire. A scar that meant I was a slave.

CHAPTER NINE

The controller made a small lump under the skin. It wasn't painful—not unless you got too close to your overseer. At ten feet, it began to feel like a slight case of indigestion. At five, it was a stone knife being twisted in your chest. Once, in an experimental mood, I pushed in to four feet from him before he noticed and waved me back. It was like a fire in my chest. That was just the mild form of its action, of course. If he had pushed the little lever on the egg-shape strapped to his arm—or died, while the thing was tuned to his body inductance—the fire in my chest would be real. Once, months later, I saw three slaves whose keeper had been accidentally killed; the holes burned in their chests from the inside were as big as dinner plates.

As a rule, though, the Lesser Triarch believed in treating his slaves well, as valuable property deserved. Hruba dropped by twice a day for the first few days to be sure that my alien flesh was healing properly. I spent my time lying on the bed or hobbling up and down the small, windowless room, talking to myself:

"You're a smart boy, Billy Danger. You learned a lot, these last four years. Enough to get yourself a ship of your own, and bring it here, against all the odds there are, to find her. And then you handed her and the ship to the midget on a silver platter—for the second time. He must have had a good laugh. For a year he followed you like a sick pup, and wagged his tail every time you looked his way. But he was waiting. And you made it easy. While you sat there poisoning yourself, he strolled back to the ship, told Huvile you weren't coming, and lifted off. The Lady Raire might have interfered, but she never knew; she didn't see you. And now Srat has her right back where she started. . . ."

It wasn't a line of thought that made me feel better, but it served the purpose of keeping me on my feet, pacing. With those ideas chewing at me, I wasn't in a mood for long, restful naps.

When the wound had stitched up, a Drathian overseer took me out of my private cell and herded me along to a big room that looked like a nineteenth century sweatshop.

There were other slaves there, forty or fifty of them, all shapes, all sizes, even a few Drathians who'd run foul of the Rule-keepers. I was assigned to a stool beside a big, broad-backed animal with a face like a Halloween mask snipped out of an old inner tube and fringed with feathery red gills. The overseers talked to him in the local buzz-buzz, and went away. He looked at me with big yellow eyes like a twin-yoked egg, and said, "Welcome to the club, friend," in perfect, unaccented lingua, in a voice that seemed to come from under a tin washtub.

He told me that his name was Fsha-fsha, that he had been left behind seventeen years before when the freighter he was shipping on had been condemned here on Drath after her linings went out, and that he had been a slave since his money ran out, three months after that.

"It's not a bad life," he said. "Plenty of food, a place to sleep, and the work's not arduous, after you've learned the routine."

The routine, he went on to explain, was Sorting. "It's a high-level job," Fsha-fsha assured me. "Only the top-category workers get this slot. And let me tell you, friend, it's better than duty in the mines, or on the pelagic harvesting rafts!"

He explained the work; it consisted of watching an endless line of glowing spheres as they came toward us along a conveyor belt, and sorting them into one of eight categories.

He told me what the types were, and demonstrated; all the while he talked, the bulbs kept
coming, and his big hands flicked the keys in
front of him, shunting them their separate
ways. But as far as I could tell, all the bulbs
were exactly alike.

"You'll learn," he said blandly, and flipped
a switch that stopped the line. He fetched a
lightweight assembly of straps from a wall
locker.

"Training harness," he explained. "It helps
you catch on in a hurry." He fitted it to me
with the straps and wires crisscrossing my
back and chest, along my arms, cinched up
tight on each finger. When he finished, he
climbed back on his stool, and switched on
the line.

"Watch," he said. The glowing bulbs came
toward him and his fingers played over the
keys.

"Now you follow through on your console,"
he said. I put my hands on the buttons and he
reached across to attach a snap that held
them there. A bulb came toward me and a sen-
sation like a hot needle stabbed the middle
finger on my right hand. I punched the key
under it and the pain stopped, but there was
another bulb coming, and the needle stabbed
my little finger this time, and I jabbed with it,
and there was another bulb coming. . . .

"It's a surefire teaching system," Fsha-fsha
said in his cheery, sub-cellar voice. "Your
hands learn to sort without even bringing the

forebrain into it. You can't beat pain-association for fast results."

For the rest of the shift, I watched glorm-bulbs sail at me, trying to second-guess the pain circuits that were activated by Fsha-fsha's selections. All I had to do was recognize a left-forefinger or right ring-finger bulb before he did, and punch the key first. By the end of the first hour my hands ached like unlanced boils. By the second hour, my arms were numb to the elbow. At the end of three hours I was throbbing all over.

"You did fine," Fsha-fsha told me when the gong rang that meant the shift was ended. "Old Hruba knew what he was doing when he assigned you here. You're a quick study. You were coding ten percent above random the last few minutes."

He took me along a damp-looking tunnel to a gloomy barracks where he and twenty-six other slaves lived. He showed me an empty alcove, got me a hammock and helped me sling it, then took me along to the mess. The cook was a warty creature with a ferocious set of ivory tusks, but he turned out to be a good-natured fellow. He cooked me up a sort of omelette that he assured me the other Man-slaves had liked. It wasn't a gourmet's delight, but it was better than the gruel I'd had in the hospital cell.

I slept then, until my new tutor shook me awake and led me back to the Sorting line.

The training sessions got worse for the next

three shifts; then I started to catch on—or my
eye and fingers did; I still couldn't con-
sciously tell one glorm-bulb from another. By
the time I'd been at it for six weeks, I was as
good as Fsha-fsha. I was promoted to a bulb-
line of my own, and the harness went back in
the locker.

The Sorting training, as it turned out, didn't
only apply to glorm-bulbs. One day the line
appeared with what looked like tangles of
colored spaghetti riding on it.

"Watch," Fsha-fsha said, and I followed
through as he sorted them into six categories.
Then I tried it, without much luck.

"You have to key-in your response
patterns," he said. "Tie this one . . ." he flipped his sorting key, ". . . to one of your
learned circuits. And this one . . ." he coded
another gob of wires, ". . . to another. . . ."

I didn't really understand all that, but I
tried making analogies to my subliminal dis-
tinctions among apparently identical glorm-
bulbs—and it worked. After that, I sorted all
kinds of things, and found that after a single
run-through, I could pick them out unerring-
ly.

"You've trained a new section of your
brain," Fsha-fsha said. "And it isn't just a
Sorting line where this works; you can use it
on any kind of categorical analysis."

During the off-shifts, we slaves were free to
relax, talk, gamble with homemade cards and
dice, commune with ourselves, or sleep.

There was a small, walled court we could crowd into when the sun shone, to soak up a little vitamin D, and a cold, sulfury-smelling cave with a pool for swimming. Some of the slaves from watery worlds spent a lot of time there. I developed a habit of taking long walks—fifty laps up and down the barrack-room—with Fsha-fsha stumping along beside me, talking. He was a great storyteller. He'd spent a hundred and thirty years in space before he'd been marooned here; he'd seen things that took the curl out of my hair to listen to.

The weeks passed and I sorted, watched, and listened. The place I was in was an underground factory, located, according to Fsha-fsha, in the heart of the city. There was only one exit, along a tunnel and up a flight of stairs barred by a steel gate that was guarded day and night.

"How do they bring in supplies?" I asked my sidekick. "How do they ship the finished products out? They can't run everything up and down one little stairway."

Fsha-fsha gave me what I had learned to interpret as a shrug. "I don't know, Danger. I've seen the stairs, because I've been out that way quite a few times—"

I stopped him and asked for a little more detail on that point.

"Now and then it happened a slave is needed for labors above-ground," he explained. "As for me, I prefer the peacefulness of my

familiar routine; still, so long as the finger of
the Triarch rests here—" he tapped a welted
purple scar along his side— "I follow all
orders with no argument."

"Listen, Fsha-fsha," I said. "Tell me everything you remember about your trips out: the
route you took, the number of guards. How
long were you out? How close did they watch
you? What kind of weapons did they carry?
Any chains or handcuffs? Many people
around? Was it day or night? Did you work inside or outside—"

"No, Danger!" Fsha-fsha waved a square
purple-palmed hand at me. "I see the way
your mind's working; but forget the idea!
Escape is impossible—and if you did break
away from a work detail, you'd still be alone
in the middle of Drath, an alien, not knowing
the language, with every Rule-keeper in the
city ready to pounce on you—"

"I know all that. But if you think I'm going
to settle down here for the rest of my life,
you're dead wrong. Now start telling me: How
many guards escorted you?"

"Just one. As long as he has my controller in
his pocket, one is all that's needed, even if I
were the most intractable slave in the pens."

"How can I get picked for an outside
detail?"

"When you're needed, you'll be called."

"Meanwhile, I'll be getting ready. Now
give."

Fsha-fsha's memory was good. I was surprised to hear that for as much as an hour at a time, he had worked unsupervised.

"It's no use creeping off and hiding out under an overturned cart or in an unused root-cellar," he said. "One touch of the controller, and you're mewling aloud for your keeper."

"That means we'll have to get our hands on the control devices before we break."

"They've thought of that; the thing is tuned to your neuronic carrier frequency. If you get within three feet of it, it's triggered automatically. If the holder dies, it's triggered. And if it's taken off of the overseer's body, the same thing."

"We can stand it long enough to smash them."

"If the controller's destroyed, you die," he said flatly. "It's covered any way you play it."

"That's where you're wrong, Fsha-fsha." I told him about crushing the controller the night I had been arrested. "Huvile didn't die. The Rule-keeper saw him board *Jongo II*, an hour afterward."

"Strange—it's common knowledge among the slaves that if your controller is damaged, it kills you."

"It's a useful story for the slave-owners to spread."

"Maybe that's why they grabbed you so fast. You might have given the game away. Hell's ice, if the slaves knew. . . ."

"How about it, Fsha-fsha? Are you with me?"

He stared at me in the gloom of the corner where we'd drifted to talk in private. "You're a strange, restless creature, Danger," he said. "For a being as frail as you are, with that soft skin and brittle bones, you've got an almighty urge to look for trouble. Why not take a tip from me and make the best of it—"

"I'll get out of here, Fsha-fsha—and get clear of the planet, too—or die trying. I'd as soon be dead as here, so I'm not risking much."

Fsha-fsha made the noise that served him as a sigh. "You know, we Rinths see the Universe differently from your Propagators," he said. "With us, it's the Great Parent that produces the spores. We workers have the mobility, the intelligence—but no future, except the Parent. We have the instinct to protect the Tree, fertilize it and water it, prune it, insure its survival; but we've got no personal stake in the future, the way you have. Your instincts tell you to stay alive and propagate. Your body knows this is a dead end as far as offspring go, so it tells you to get out or die." He sighed again. "When I left Rinth, it was hard; for a long time, I had a homesickness that you wouldn't be able to understand—any more than I can really understand the way you feel now. But I can remember how it was. And if it's anything like that with you—yes; I can see you've got to try."

"That's right; I've got to try. But not you,

Fsha-fsha. If you're really content here, stay. I'll make it on my own."

"You wouldn't have a chance, Danger. I know the language, the routes around the town. You need me. Not that it'll do any good in the end. But knowing about the controllers will make a difference."

"Forget it. You can teach me the language, and tell me all you can about the town. But there's no point in your getting killed—"

"That's another advantage a Rinth has," Fsha-fsha cut me off. "No instinct for self-pre-servation. Now, let's get started planning the details."

The weeks went by. I sorted, slept, took my language lesson, and worked to memorize the map of the city I drew up from Fsha-fsha's descriptions. About two months after our decision to crash out, Fsha-fsha got a call for an outside detail. He vetoed my suggestion that I volunteer to go along.

"This is a lucky break," he said. "It will give me a chance to look over the ground again, in the light of our plans. Rest easy. We'll get our chance."

"We Propagators aren't as patient as you Tree-farmers," I told him. "It may be another six months before an outside detail comes up again."

"Better to propagate in your old age than not at all, eh?" he reminded me, and I had to bite my teeth and watch him go. I got one quick look at the passage as he left. It was narrow, dim-lit; the Drathians didn't like a high level of illumination. I wondered if there was a useful tip for me in that.

Fsha-fsha came back rippling his gill-flaps in a way that I knew meant he was excited. But it turned out not to be pleased anticipation.

"It's hopeless, Danger," he assured me. "The Wormface in charge of the detail carries the controllers in a special rack, strapped to his chest for quick access. He keeps his distance; ten feet was as close as I could get before he warned me back."

"What weapons did he carry?" I asked him.

"What weapon does he need? He holds your life in his hand as it is!"

"Too bad," I said. "We'll have to get our armaments somewhere else then."

Fsha-fsha goggled at me. "You're an amazing creature, Danger. If you were cornered by a Fangmaster, I think you'd complain that his teeth weren't larger, so as to provide you with a better dagger!"

The routine settled in again then. Every day was like the one before; the glorm-bulbs rushed at me in a stream that never ended, never changed. I ate omelettes, played revo and tikal and a dozen other games, walked my two miles a day, up and down the dark room; and waited. And one day, I made a blunder that ended our plans with total finality.

The work-shift had ended half an hour before. Fsha-fsha and I had settled down in his alcove to play our favorite game of telling each other what we'd do, once we were clear of Drath. A big Drathian slave who'd been assigned to the Sorting crew a few hours earlier came lumbering over, breathing out fumes that reminded me of a package of rotten broccoli I'd opened once by mistake.

"I'll take this alcove," he said to Fsha-fsha. "Get out, animal."

"Makes himself right at home, doesn't he?" I pointed across the room to an empty alcove. "Try over there, sport," I said to the broccoli-breather. "Lots of room—" I got that far when he reached out with a couple of arms like boa constrictors and ripped down the hammock. He yanked again, and tore the other end free. He tossed it aside and swung his own kit down onto the floor. I stood up.

"Wait," Fsha-fsha said quickly. "The overseer will deal with this one. Don't—"

The big Drathian took a quick step, threw a punch at me. I ducked, came up with a three-foot length of steel pipe the Rinth had tucked under the hammock for possible future use, and brought it down in a two-handed blow across the Drathian's shoulder. He gave a bleat like a branded steer and went down bucking and kicking. In his convulsion, he beat his head against the floor, whipped his body against the wall hard enough to give off a dull *boom!* like a whale slapping the water with its tail. Thick, yellowish blood spattered. Every slave in the barracks came crowding around to see what was going on, but in thirty seconds it was all over. The big Drathian was dead. The Rule-keepers got there a minute or two later and took me away, up the stairs I'd looked forward to seeing for so long.

My hearing didn't amount to much. I explained to Hruba that the dead slave had attacked me, that I didn't know Drathians kept their brains under their shoulder blades; but it was an open-and-shut case. I'd killed a fellow slave. My Sorting days were over.

"Transporation to the harvesting rafts," the majordomo intoned in Drathian and repeated it in lingua. "Too bad, Man," he added in his unofficial voice. "You were a valuable Sorter—but like your kind, you have a savage streak in you most unbecoming in a chattel."

They clamped my wrists in a steel ring and hustled me out into a courtyard where a big, tarry-smelling air-barge was waiting. I climbed aboard, and was kicked into a metal-walled broom-closet. They slammed the door on me, and I lay in the dark and felt the barge lift off.

The harvesting rafts were mile-square constructions of metal floats linked by woven-rope mats and carpeted with rotting vegetable husks and the refuse of the canning sheds, which worked night and day processing the marine life hoisted aboard by the seining derricks. A pair of husky Drathians threw me off the side of the barge into foul-odored ankle-deep muck, and another pair grabbed me, knocked me around a little just to keep in practice, and dragged me away to a long lean-to which served to keep the worst of the sub-tropical rains off any of the workers who were lucky enough to be on off-shift. They took off the wrist-irons and rigged a fine-gauge fiber loop around my neck, not tight enough to choke me, but plenty snug enough to wear the skin raw, until it toughened and formed a half-inch-wide scar that itched and burned day and night. There was a limp bladder attached to the rope, designed to inflate and keep my head above water if I happened to fall overboard; slaves weren't allowed to evade their labors by anything as easy as drowning, intentionally or otherwise. I learned all this later; the first night the only orientation I got was what I could deduce from being dragged to a line of workers who were shelling out big crustaceans, and yelled at to get to work. The command was emphasized with a kick, but I had been watching for that; I slid aside from it and smashed my fist into the short ribs of the Drathian and chopped him again as he scrambled back. My reward for this effort was a solid beating, administered by three Drathians, two holding and one swinging a rod as heavy and limber as a golf club. They finished after a while, threw water over me, and someone shoved a sea-lobster at me.

"Better look busy," the slave on my left tipped me off. He was a medium-sized Drathian with a badly scarred face; that made us pals on two counts. I followed his advice.

There wasn't anything complicated about the work; you grabbed your chzik, held him by the blunt end, hooked a finger under his carapace, and stripped it off him. Then you captured his four flailing limbs, and with a neat twist of wrist, removed them. The chziks were active creatures, and they showed their resentment of this treatment by writhing frantically during the operation. When you found yourself tackling a big fellow—weight ten pounds or more—it could sometimes be a

little difficult to carry out the job as smoothly
as the overseers desired. They usually let you
know when this was the case by hitting you
across the back with the golf club.

At first, my fingers had a tendency to bleed,
since the carapaces were razor-sharp and as
tough as plexiglass, and the barbs on the legs
had a way of lodging in my palms. But the
wounds healed cleanly; the microorganisms
of Drath were too alien to my metabolism to
give rise to infections. And after a while
calluses formed.

I was lucky in timing my arrival near the
end of a shift; I was able to look busy enough
to keep the overseer away, and make it under
my own power to the shed. There were no
bunks, no assigned spaces. You just crowded
in as far as possible from the weather side
and dropped. There was no insomnia on the
rafts. The scarred Drathian—the same one
who had given me some good advice the first
night—helped me out again the next shift, by
showing me how to nip off a chunk of raw
chzik and suck it for the water content. The
meat itself was spongy and inedible as far as I
was concerned; but the slop dipped up to us at
the regular feeding time was specially designed to be assimilable by a wide variety of
species. When an off-brand worker showed up
who couldn't live on the stuff, he soon star-
ved, thus solving the problem.

Instead of the regular cycle of alternating
work- and rest-shifts, we harvesters worked

two shifts out of three, which effectively pre-
vented any chance of boredom. For six hours
at a stretch, we manned our places by the
chute with the squirming heaps of chziks arriving just a little faster than we could shell
them out. The slippery mat under foot rose
and fell in its never-ending rhythm, and beyond its edge, the steel-gray sea stretched to
the horizon. Sometimes the sun beat down in
a dead calm, and the unbelievable stink rose
around us like a foul tide. At night floodlights
glared from high on the derricks, and the in-
sects swarmed in to fly into our mouths and
eyes and be trampled underfoot to add to the
carpet. Sometimes rain came, hot and torrent-
ial, but the line never slowed. And later, when
gray sleet coated the rigging and decks with
soft ice, and the wind cut at us like sabers, we
worked on, those of us who could stand the
cold, the others settled into the muck and
were hauled away and put over the side. And
some of us who were still alive envied them.

I remembered reading, years before, back
on old Earth of concentration camp pris-
oners, and I wondered what it was that kept
men going under conditions that made life a
torture that never ended. Now I knew; it
wasn't a high-minded determination to endure, or a dauntless will to take a blood-
curdling revenge. It was an instinct older than
thought, older than hate, that said: "Survive!"

And I survived. My hands toughened, my
muscles strengthened, my skin hardened

against the cold and the rain. I learned to sleep in icy slush, without protection, with horny feet stumbling over me in the dark; to swallow the watery gruel and hold out the cup for more; to take the routine club-blows of the overseers without hitting back; in the end, without really noticing. There were no friendships on the rafts, no recreations. There was no time or energy for anything not directly related to staying alive for one more day. The Drathian who had helped me on the first day died one wet night, and another took his place; I had never even learned his name.

During my years in space, I had developed an instinctive time-sense that told me when a week, or a month, Earth-style, had passed. I had been almost five years away, now. Sometimes I wondered what had happened during those years, back on that small planet. But it was so far away that it seemed more like a dream than a reality.

For hours at a stretch, sometimes for a whole double shift, my mind would wander far away from the pelagic rafts of Drath. My memories seemed to become more vivid with time, until they were almost realer than the meaningless life around me.

And then one night, the routine broke. A morose-looking Drathian boss-overseer caught me as I went toward the chzik chute, shoved me toward the boat wharf.

"You're assigned as a net-handler," he told me. Except for the heavy leather coat he was

wearing, he looked as cold and filthy and mis-
erable as the slaves. I climbed down into the
twenty-foot, double-prowed dory that was
pitching in the choppy water at the foot of the
loading ladder, and we shoved off. In five
minutes the high-sided raft was out of sight in
the ragged fog.

I sat in the stern and stared at the oily gray
surface of the water. It was the first new sight
I'd seen in many months. The wake was a
swirl of foam that drifted aft, forming a pattern like an ugly face that leered up at me
through the murky water. The face grew
clearer, and then it broke water, a devil-mask
of rippling black leaves edged with feathery
red gills. An arm swept up, dripping water; I
saw the flash of a knife blade as it swept down
toward me—and felt the rope fall from my
neck. A wide hand clamped on my arm, tumbled me over the stern, and before I could draw
a breath, had dragged me down into the cold
and the dark.

I woke up lying on my back in a warm, dry
place. From the motion and the sound, I could
tell I was on a boat. The air that moved over
my face carried the sweet, clean smell of the
sea. Fsha-fsha was standing beside the bunk;

in the soft glow from the deck lamp, his face looked almost benign.

"It's a good thing I recognized you," I said, and was surprised at the weakness of my voice. "I might have spoiled things by putting a thumb in your eye."

"Sorry about the rough treatment," he said. "It was the best we could work out. The tender-master wasn't in on it; just the boss-overseer."

"It worked," I said, and stopped to cough, and tasted the alien saltwater of Drath. "That's all that counts."

"We're not clear yet, but the trickiest part went all right. Maybe the rest will work out, too."

"Where are we headed?"

"There's an abandoned harbor not far from here; about four hours' run. A flier will meet us there." I started to ask another question, but my eye was too heavy to hold open. I closed it and the warm blanket of darkness folded in on me.

Voices woke me. For a moment, I was back aboard Lord Desroy's yacht, lying on a heap of uncured *Nith*-hides, and the illusion was so strong that I felt a ghostly pang from the arm, broken and mended so long ago. Then Fsha-fsha's voice cut through the dream.

". . . up now, Danger, have to walk a little way. How do you feel?"

I sat up and put my legs over the side of the cot and stood. "Like a drowned sailor," I said. "Let's go."

Up on the deck of the little surface cutter, I could see lights across the water. Fsha-fsha had put a heavy mackinaw across my shoulders. For the first time in a year, I felt cold. The engines idled back and we swung in beside a jetty. A small, furtive-looking Drathian was waiting beside a battered cargo-car. We climbed up into the box and settled down under some stiff tarpaulins, and a moment later the truck started up and pulled out in a whine of worn turbos.

I slept again. The habit of almost a year on the rafts, to sleep whenever I wasn't on the line, was too strong to break in an hour; and breathing the salt seas of Drath isn't the best treatment for human lungs. When I woke up this time, the car had stopped. Fsha-fsha put a hand on my arm and I lay quiet. Then he tapped me and we crawled out and slid down the tailgate, and I saw we were parked at the edge of the spaceport at Drath City. The big dome loomed up under the black sky across the ramp, as faded and patched as ever; and between us and it, the clumsy bulk of an ancient cargo-carrier squatted on battered parking jacks.

Something moved in the shadows and a cur-
iously shaped creature swathed in a long
cloak came up to us. He flipped back the hood
and I saw the leathery face of a Rithian.

"You're late," he said unhurriedly. "A
couple of local gendarmes nosing about. Best
we waste no time." He turned and moved off
toward the freighter. Fsha-fsha and I followed. We had covered half the distance when an
actinic-green floodlight speared out to etch us
in light, and a rusty-hinged voice shouted the
Drathian equivalent of "Halt or I'll shoot!"

I ran for it. The Rithian, ten feet in the lead,
spun, planted himself, brought up his arm
and a vivid orange light winked. The spotlight
flared and died, and I was past him, sprinting
for the open cargo-port, still a hundred yards
away across open pavement. A gun stuttered
from off to the right, where the searchlight
had been, and in the crisp yellow flashes I saw
Drathian Rule-keepers bounding out to intercept us.

I altered course and charged the nearest
Rule-keeper, hit him fair and square. As he
fell, my fingers, which had learned to strip the
carapace from a twelve-pound chzik with one
stroke, found his throat and cartilage crumpled and popped and he went limp and I was

back on my feet in time to see the other Drathian lunge for Fsha-fsha. I took him from behind, broke his neck with my forearm, lifted
him and threw him ten feet from me. And we
were running again.

The open port was just ahead, a brilliant
rectangle against the dark swell of the hulk.
Something gleamed red there, and Fsha-fsha
threw himself sideways and a ravening spout
of green fire lanced out and I went flat and
rolled and saw a giant Drathian, his white
serape thrown back across his shoulder,
swinging a flare-muzzled gun around to cover
me. I came to my feet and dove straight at
him, but I knew I wouldn't make it—

Something small and dark plunged from
the open port, leaped to the Drathian's back.
He twisted, struck down with the butt of the
gun, and I heard it thud on flesh. He struck
again, and bone crunched, and the small, dark
thing fell away, twisting on the pavement; and
then I was on the Rule-keeper. I caught the
gun muzzle, ripped it out of his hands, threw
it away into the dark. His face was coming
around to me, and I swung with all the power
that the months of mule-labor had given my
arm, and felt the horny mask collapse, saw
the ochre blood spatter; he went down and I
stepped over him and the small, dark creature
that had attacked him moved and the light
from the entry fell across it and showed me
the mangled body of a H'eeaq.

Up above, a shrill Rithian voice was shouting. Behind me, I heard the thud of Drathian feet, their sharp, buzzing commands.

"Srat," I said, and could say no more. Thick, blackish blood welled from ghastly wounds. Broken rib-ends projected from the warty hide of his chest. One great goggle-eye was knocked from its socket. The other held on me.

"Master," the ugly voice croaked. "Greatly . . . my people wronged you. Yet—if my wounds . . . may atone for yours . . . forego your vengeance . . . for they are lonely . . . and afraid. . . ."

"Srat . . . I thought . . ."

"I fought the Man, Master," he gasped out. "But he . . . was stronger . . . than I. . . ."

"Huvile!" I said. "*He* took the ship!"

Srat made a convulsive movement. He tried to speak, but only a moan came from his crocodile mouth.

I leaned closer.

"I die, Master," he said, "obedient . . . to your . . . desires. . . ."

CHAPTER TEN

Fsha-fsha and a Rishian crewman hauled me aboard the ship; Srat's corpse was left on the ramp. Other species aren't as sentimental about such things as Man is. There were a few angry objections from Drath Traffic Control as we lifted, but the Drathians had long since given up Deep Space travel, and the loss of a couple of runaway slaves wasn't sufficient reason to alienate the Rishians. They were one of the few worlds that still sent tramps into Fringe Space.

Once away, Fsha-fsha told me all that had happened since I was sent to the rafts:

"Once you'd planted the idea of escape, I had to go ahead with it," he said. "The next chance was three months later, two of us this time, just one overseer. I had a fancy plan worked out for decoying him into a side alley, but I had a freak piece of luck. It was a loading job, and a net broke and scattered cargo all over the wharf. The other slave got the whole load on his head—and a nice-sized iron casting clipped the guard and laid him out cold. He had the controllers strapped to his arm, in plain sight, but getting to them was the hardest thing I ever did in my life. I used a metal bar from the spilled cargo on them and fainted at the same time.

"I came out of it just in time. The Loadmaster and a couple of Rule-keepers were just arriving. I got up and ran for it. They wasted a little time discovering my controller was out of action, and by then I had a good start. I headed for a hideaway I'd staked out earlier, and laid up there until dark.

"That night I came out and took a chance on a drinking-house that was run by a non-Drathian. I thought maybe he'd have a little sympathy for a fellow alien. I was wrong, but I strapped him to the bed and filled both my stomachs with high-lipid food, enough to keep me going for two weeks, and took what cash he had in the place and got clear.

"With money to spend, things were a little easier. I found a dive where I could lie low, no questions asked, and sent out feelers for information on where you'd been sent. The next day the little guy showed up: Srat.

"He'd been hanging around, waiting for a chance to talk to someone from the Triarch's stable. I don't know what he'd been eating, but it wasn't much; and he slept in the street.

"I told him what I knew; between us, we got you located. Then the Rish ship showed up."

The Rishian captain was sitting with us, listening. He wrinkled his face at me.

"The H'eeaq, Srat, spoke to me in my own tongue, greatly to my astonishment. Long ago, at Rish, I'd heard the tale of the One-Eyed Man who'd bartered half of the light of his world for the lives of his fellows. The symmetry of the matter demanded that I give such a one the help he asked."

"The little guy didn't look like much," Fsha-fsha said. "But he had all the guts there were."

"You may take pleasure in the memory of that rarest of creatures," the Rishian said. "A loyal slave."

"He was something rarer than that," I said. "A friend."

Fsha-fsha and I stayed with the freighter for three months; we left her on a world called Gloy. We could have ridden her all the way to Rith, but my destination was in the opposite direction: Zeridajh. Fsha-fsha stayed with me. One world was like another to him, he said. As for the ancestral Tree, having cut the ties, like a man recovered from an infatuation, he wasn't eager to retie them. The Rish captain paid us off for our services aboard his vessel—we had rebuilt his standby power section, as well as pulling regular shifts with the crew. That gave us enough cash to reoutfit ourselves with respectable clothes and take rooms at a decent inn near the port, while we looked for a Center-bound berth.

We had a long wait, but it could have been worse. There were shops and taverns and apartments built among the towering ruins of a vast city ten thousand years dead; but the ruins were overgrown and softened by time, so that the town seemed to be built among forested hills, unless you saw it from the air and realized that the mountains were vine-grown structures.

There was work for us on Gloy; by living frugally and saving what we earned, we accumulated enough for passenger berths inward to Tanix, a crossroads world where the volume of in-Galaxy shipping was more encouraging. After a few days' wait, we signed on a mile-long super-liner. It was a four months' cruise; at the end of it we stepped off on the soil of a busy trading planet, and looked up at the blaze of sky that meant Center was close.

"It's still three thousand lights run to Zeri-dajh," the Second Officer for Power told me as he paid me off. "Why not sign on for another cruise? Good powermen are hard to find; I can offer you a nice bonus."

"It's useless, Second," Fsha-fsha answered for me. "Danger is searching for a magic flower that only grows in one special garden, at the hub of the Galaxy."

After a couple of weeks of job-hunting, we signed on as scrapers on a Center-bound tub crewed by small, damp dandies from the edge of Center. That was the only berth a highbrow Center skipper would consider handing a barbarian from what they called the Outworlds. It was a long cruise, and as far as I could tell, the jobs that fell to a scraper on a Center ship were just as dirty as on any Outworld tub.

On our next cruise, we found ourselves stranded on a backwater world by a broken-down guidance system on the rotting hulk we had shipped in on. We waited for a berth outbound for a month, then took service under a local constabulary boss as mercenaries. We did a lot of jumping around the planet, marching in ragged jungle and eating inedible rations, and in the end barely got clear with our hides intact when the constabulary turned out to be a daciot force. I made one interesting discovery; my sorting skill came in handy in using the bill-hook machetes issued to the troops. After one or two small run-ins, I had keyed-in a whole set of reflex responses that made me as good as the battalion champion.

Usually, though, we didn't see much of the planets we visited. It was normal practice, all across the Galaxy, for a world to channel all its space-faring commerce and traffic through a single port, for economy of facilities and ease of control. The ports I saw were like ports in all times and climes: cities without personality, reduced to the lowest common denominator of the thousand breeds of being they served.

After that, we found another slot, and another after that, on a small, fast lugger from Thlinthor; and on that jump we had a change in luck.

I was sound asleep in the off-watch cubbyhole I rated as a scraper when the alarm sirens went off. It took me thirty seconds to roll out and get across the deck to the screens where Fsha-fsha and half a dozen other onwatch crewmen were gaping at a sight that you only see once in a lifetime in Deep Space: a derelict hulk, adrift among the stars. This one was vast—and you could tell at one glance that she was old. . . .

We were five hundred miles apart, closing on courses that were only slightly skew; that made two miracles. We hove-to ten miles from her and took a good look, while the power officer conferred with Command Deck. Then the word came through to resume course.

"Huh?" Both Fsha-fsha and I swiveled on him. From the instant I'd seen the hulk, visions of prize-money had been dancing in my head like sugarplums. "He's not going to salvage her?" Fsha-fsha came as close to yelling as his mild nature would let him.

The power officer gave him a fishy look from fishy eyes in a fishy face. Like the rest of the crew, he was an amphibian who slept in a tank of salty water for three hours at a stretch—and like all his tribe, he was an agoraphobe to the last feathery scale on his rudimentary rudder fin. "It ith not practical," he said coldly.

"That tub's fifty thousand years old if she's a day," Fsha-fsha protested. "And I'm a mud-puppy if she's not a Riv Surveyor! She'll be loaded with Pre-collapse star maps! There'll be data aboard her that's been lost since before Thlinthor lofted her first satellite!"

"How would you propoth that we acthelerate thuch a math as that to interthtellar velothity?" he put the question to us. "The hulk outweighth uth a million to one. Our engines were not dethigned for thuch threthes."

"She looks intact," I said. "Maybe her engines are still in working order."

"Tho?"

"We can put a prize crew aboard her and

bring her in under her own power."

The Thlinthorian tucked his head down between his shoulder plates, his version of a
shudder.

"We Thlinthorians have no tathte for thuch
exthploiths," he said. "Our mithion is the
thafe delivery of conthigned cargo—"

"You don't have to go out on the hull," Fsha-
fsha said. "Danger and I will volunteer."

The power officer goggled his eyes at us and
conferred with Command Deck. After a few
minutes of talk word came through that his
Excellency the Captain was agreeable.

"One stipulation," I said. "We'll do the dirty
work; but we take a quarter-share between
us."

The captain made a counter-offer of a twen-
tieth share each. We compromised on a tenth.

"I don't like it," Fsha-fsha told me. "He gave
in too easily."

We suited up and took a small boat across
to the old ship. She was a glossy brown ovoid
about half a mile in diameter. Matching up
with her was like landing on a planetoid. We
found a hatch and a set of outside controls
that let us into a dusty, cavernous hold. From
there we went on through passenger quarters,
recreation areas, technical labs and program
rooms. In what looked like an armory, Fsha-
fsha and I looked over a treasure-house of
sophisticated personal offense and defense
devices. Everything was in perfect order; and

nowhere, then or later, did we ever find a bone of her crew, or any hint of what had happened to her.

A call from the captain on the portable communicator reminded us sharply that we had a job to do.

We followed a passage big enough to drive a moving van through, found the engine room, about the size of Grand Central Station. The generators ranged down the center of it were as massive as four-story apartment buildings. I whistled when I saw them, but Fsha-fsha took it in stride.

"I've seen bigger," he said. "Let's check out the system."

It took us four hours to work out the meaning of the oversized controls ranged in a circular console around a swiveled chair the size of a bank vault. But the old power plant started up with as sweet a rumble as if it had been in use every day.

After a little experimental jockeying, I got the big hull aligned on course coordinates and fed the power to the generators. As soon as we were up to cruise velocity, His Excellency the Captain ordered us back aboard. "Who are you sending over to relieve us?" I asked him.

"You may leave that detail to my discrethion," he told me in a no-argument tone.

"I can't leave this power section unmanned," I said.

He bugged his eyes at me on the four-inch

screen of the pocket communicator and repeated his order, louder, with quotations
from the Universal Code.

"I don't like it," Fsha-fsha said. "But I'm
afraid we haven't got much choice."

Back aboard the mother-ship, our reception
was definitely cool. Word had gotten around
that we'd pigged an extra share of the goodies.
That suited me all right. The Thlinthorians
weren't the kind who inspired much in the
way of affection.

When we were well inside the Thlinthorian
system the power officer called Fsha-fsha and
me in and showed us what was probably a
smile.

"I confeth I entertained a thertain thuth-
pithion of you both," he confided. "But now
that we have arrived in the Home Thystem
with our thuperb prize thafely in the thlave
orbit, I thee that my cauthion was exthethive.
Gentlemen, join me in a drink!"

We accepted the invitation, and he poured
out nice-sized tumblers of wine. I was just
reaching for mine when Fsha-fsha jostled the
table and sloshed wine from the glasses. The
power officer waved aside his apologies and
turned to ring for a mess-boy to mop up the
puddle. In the instant his back was turned,
Fsha-fsha dropped a small pellet in our host's
drink, where it dissolved instantly. We all sat
smiling benignly at each other while the small
Thlinthorian servant mopped up, then lifted
our glasses and swallowed. Fsha-fsha gulped

his down whole. I took a nice swallow of mine, nodded my appreciation and took another. Our host chugalugged and poured another round. We sipped this one; he watched us and we watched him. I saw his eyes wander to the time-scale on the wall. Fsha-fsha looked at it, too.

"How long does it take your stuff to work?" he inquired pleasantly of the Thlinthorian. The latter goggled his eyes, made small choking noises, then, in a strangled voice said: "A quarter of an hour."

Fsha-fsha nodded. "I can feel it, a little," he said. "We both belted a couple of null-pills before we came up, just in case you had any funny stuff you wanted to try. How do you feel?"

"Not well," the fish-mouth swallowed air. "I cannot control . . . my thpeech!"

"Right. Now, tell us all about everything. Take your time. It'll be an hour or two before we hit Planetary Control. . . ."

Fsha-fsha and I reached the port less than ten minutes behind the boat we had trailed in from where our ship and the Riv vessel were parked, a hundred thousand miles out. We found the captain already at the mutual-congratulation stage with the portmaster. His already prominent eyes nearly rolled down his scaled cheeks when he saw us.

"Perhaps the captain forgot to mention that he owes Captain Danger and myself a tenth-share in the prize," Fsha-fsha said, after the introductions were over.

"That's a prepothterouth falthhood!" the officer started, but Fsha-fsha cut him off by producing a pocket recorder of a type allowable in every law court in the Bar. The scene that followed lacked that sense of close comradeship so desirable in captain-crew relationships, but there was nothing our former commander could do but go along.

Afterward, in the four-room suite we treated ourselves to to rest up in, Fsha-fsha said, "Ah, by the way, Danger, I happened to pick up a little souvenir aboard that Riv tub—" He did something complicated with the groont-hide valise he carried his personal gear in and took out a small packet which opened out into a crisscross of flat, black straps with a round pillbox in the center.

"I checked it out," he said, sounding like a kid with a new bike. "This baby is something: A personal body shield. Wear it under your tunic. Sets up a field nothing gets through!"

"Nifty," I agreed, and worked the slides on the bottom of my kit bag. "*I* took a fancy to *this* little jewel." I held up my memento. It was a very handsome wristlet, which just fit around my neck.

"Uh-huh, pretty," Fsha-fsha said. "This harness of mine is so light you don't know you're wearing it—"

"It's not only pretty, it's a sense-booster," I interrupted his paean. "It lowers the stimulus-response threshold for sight, hearing and touch."

"I guess we out-traded old Slinth-face after all," Fsha-fsha said, after we'd each checked out the other's keepsake. "This squares the little finesse he tried with the sleepy-pills."

The salvage authorities made us wait around for almost a month, but since they were keeping forty Thlinthorian crew members waiting, too, in the end they had to publish the valuation and pay off all hands. Between us, Fsha-fsha and I netted more cash than the lifetime earnings of a spacer.

We shipped out the same day, a short hop to Hrix, a human-occupied world in a big twenty-seven-planet system only half a light from Thlinthor. It seemed like a good idea not to linger around town after the payoff. On Hrix, we shopped for a vessel of our own; something small, and superfast. We still had over two thousand lights to cover.

Hrix was a good place to ship-hunt. It had been a major shipbuilding world for a hundred thousand years, since before the era known as the Collapse when the original Central Empire folded—and incidentally gave the upstart tribe called Man its chance to spread out over the Galaxy.

For two weeks we looked at brand-new

ships, good-as-new second- and third- and
tenth-hand jobs, crawled over hulls, poked
into power sections, kicked figurative tires in
every shipyard in town, and were no further
along than the day we started. The last evening, Fsha-fsha and I were at a table under the
lanterns swinging from the low branches of
the Heo trees in the drinking garden attached
to our inn, talking over the day's frustrations.

"These new hulls we've been looking at,"
Fsha-fsha said; "mass-produced junk; not like
the good old days—"

"The old stuff isn't much, either," I countered. "They were built to last, and at those
crawl-speeds, they had to."

"Anything we can afford, we don't want,"
Fsha-fsha summed it up. "And anything we
want, costs too much."

The landlord who was refilling our wine jug
spoke up. "If you gentlebeings are looking for
something a little out of the usual line, I have
an old grand-uncle—fine old chap, full of lore
about old times—he's over three hundred you
know—who still dabbles in buying and sell-
ing. There's a hull in his yard that might be
just what the sirs are looking for, with a little
fixing up—"

We managed to break into the pitch long
enough to find out where the ship was, and
after emptying our jug, took a walk down
there. It looked like every junkyard I've ever
seen. The place was grown with weeds taller
than I was, and the sales office was a salvaged

escape blister, with flowers growing in little clay pots in the old jet orifices. There was a light on, though, and we pounded until an old crookbacked fellow with a few wisps of pink hair and a jaw like a snapping turtle poked his head out. We explained what we wanted, and who had sent us. He cackled and rubbed his hands and allowed as how we'd come to the right place. By this time we were both thinking we'd made a mistake. There was nothing here but junk so old that even the permalloy was beginning to corrode. But we followed him back between towering stacks of obsolete parts and assemblies, over heaps of warped hull-plates, through a maze of stacked atmosphere fittings to what looked like a thicket dense enough for Bre'r Rabbit to hide in.

"If you sirs'll just pull aside a few tendrils of that danged wire vine," the old boy suggested. Fsha-fsha had his mouth open to decline, but out of curiosity, I started stripping away a finger-thick creeper, and back in the green-black gloom I saw a curve of dull-polished metal. Fsha-fsha joined in, and in five minutes we had uncovered the stern of what had once been elegance personified.

"She was built by Sanjio," the oldster told us. "See there?" he pointed at an ornate emblem, still jewel-bright against the tarnished metal. Fsha-fsha ran his hand over curve of the boat's flank, peered along the slim-lined hull. Our eyes met.

"How much?" he asked.

"You'll put her in shape, restore her," the old man said. "You wouldn't cut her up for the heavy metal in her jump fields, or convert her for rock-prospecting." It was a question. We both yelled no loud enough to safisfy him.

The old man nodded. "I like you boys' looks," he said. "I wouldn't sell her to just anybody. She's yours."

It took us a day to cut the boat free of the growth that had been crawling over her for eighty years. The old man, whose name was Knoute, managed, with curses and pleas and some help from a half-witted lad named Dune, to start up a long-defunct yard-tug and move the boat into a cleared space big enough to give us access to her. Fsha-fsha and I went through her from stem to stern. She was complete, original right down to the old logbook still lying in the chart table. It gave us some data to do further research on. I spent an afternoon in the shipping archives in the city, and that evening at dinner read the boat's history to Fsha-fsha:

"*Gleerim*, fifty-five feet, one hundred and nine tons. Built by Sanjio, master builder to Prince Ahax, as color-bearer to the Great House, in the year Qon. . . ."

"That would be just over four thousand years ago," Knoute put in.

"In her maiden year, the Prince Ahax raced her at Poylon, and at Gael, and led a field of thirty-two to win at Fonteraine. In her fortieth year, with a long record of brilliant victories affixed to her crestplate, the boat was sold at auction by the hard-pressed and aged prince. Purchased by a Vidian dealer, she was passed on to the Solarch of Trie, whose chief of staff, recognizing the patrician lines of the vessel, refitted her as his personal scout. Captured nineteen years later in a surprise raid by the Alzethi, the boat was mounted on a wooden-wheeled platform and hauled by chained dire-beasts in a triumphal procession through the streets of Alz. Thereafter, for more than a century, the boat lay abandoned on her rotting cart at the edge of the noisome town.

"Greu of Balgreu found the forgotten boat, and set a crew to cutting her out of her bed of tangled wildwood. Fancying the vessel's classic lines, the invading chieftain removed her to a field depot, where his shipfitters hammered in vain at her locked port. Greu himself hacked in at her crestplate, desiring it as an ornament, but succeeded only in shattering his favorite dress short-sword. In his rage, he ordered flammable rubble to be heaped on the boat, soaked with volatiles, and fired. After he razed the city and departed with his troops, the boat again lay in neglect for two centuries. Found by the Imperial Survey Team of his Effulgent Majesty, Lleon the fortieth, she was returned to Ahax, where she was refitted and returned to service as color-bearer to the Imperial House.''

"That was just her first days," Knoute said. "She's been many places since then, seen many sights. And the vessel doesn't exist to this day that can outrun her.''

It took us three months to repair, refit, clean, polish, tune and equip the boat to suit ourselves and old Knoute. But in the end even he had to admit that the Prince Ahax himself couldn't have done her more proud. And when the time came to pay him, he waved the money aside.

"I won't live to spend it," he said. "And you boys have bled yourselves white, doing her up. You'll need what you've got left to cruise her as she should be cruised, wanting nothing. Take her, and see that the lines you add to her log don't shame her history.''

Two thousand light-years is a goodly distance, even when you're riding the ravening stream of raw power that *Jongo III* ripped out of the fabric of the continuum and converted to acceleration that flung us inward at ten, a hundred, a thousand times the velocity of propagation of radiation. We covered the distance in jumps of a month or more, while the blaze of stars thickened across the skies ahead like clotting cream. We saw worlds where intelligent life had existed for thousands of centuries, planets that were the graveyards of cultures older than the dinosaurs of Earth. When our funds ran low, we made the discovery that even here at the heart of the Galaxy, there were people who would pay us a premium for fast delivery of passengers and freight.

Along the way we encountered life-forms that ranged from intelligent gnat-swarms to the titanic slumbering swamp-minds of Buroom. We found men on a hundred worlds, some rugged pioneers barely holding their own against hostile environments of ice or desert or competing flora and fauna, others the polished and refined products of millenia-old empires that had evolved cultural machinery as formal and complex as a life-long ballet. There were worlds where we were welcomed to cities made of jade and crystal, and worlds where sharpers with faces like Neapolitan street-urchins plotted to rob and kill us; but our Riv souvenirs served us well, and a certain instinct for survival got us through.

And the day came when Zeridajh swam into our forward screens, a misty green world with two big moons.

The Port of Radaj was a multilevel composition of gardens, pools, trees, glass-smooth paving, sculpture-clean facades, with the transient shipping parked on dispersed pads like big toys set out for play. Fsha-fsha and I dressed up in our best shore-going clothes and rode a toy train in to a country-club style terminal.

The landing formalities were minimal; a gray-haired smoothie who reminded me of an older Sir Orfeo welcomed us to the planet, handed us illuminated handmaps, that showed us our position as a moving point of green light, and asked how he could be of service.

"I'd like to get news of someone," I told him. "A Lady—the Lady Raire."

"Of what house?"

"I don't know; but she was traveling in the company of Lord Desroy."

He directed us to an information center that turned out to be manned by a computer. After a few minutes of close questioning and a display of triograms, the machine voice advised me that the lady I sought was of the House of Ancinet-Chanore, and that an interview with the head of the house would be my best bet for further information.

"But is she here?" I pressed the point. "Did she get back home safely?"

The computer repeated its advice and added that transportation was available outside gate twelve.

We crossed the wide floor of the terminal and came out on a platform where a gorgeous scarlet and silver inlaid porcelain car waited. We climbed in, and a discreet voice whispered an inquiry as to our destination.

"The Ancinet-Chanore estate," I told it, and it clicked and whooshed away along a curving, soaring avenue that lofted us high above wooden hills and rolling acres of lawn with glass-smooth towers in pastel colors pushing up among the crowns of multi-thousand-year-old Heo trees. After a fast half-hour run, the car swooped down an exit ramp and pulled up in front of an imposing gate. A gray-liveried man on duty there asked us a few questions, played with a console inside his glass-walled cubicle, and advised us that the Lord Pastaine was at leisure and would be happy to grant us an interview.

"Sounds like a real VIP," Fsha-fsha commented as the car tooled up the drive and deposited us at the edge of a terrace fronting a sculptured facade.

"Maybe it's just a civilized world," I suggested.

Another servitor in gray greeted us and ushered us inside, through a wide hall where sunlight slanting down through a faceted ceiling shed a rosy glow on luminous wood and brocaded hangings, winked from polished sculp-

tures perched in shadowy recesses. And I
thought of the Lady Raire, coming from this,
living in a cave grubbed out of a dirk-bank,
singing to herself as she planted wild flowers
along the paths. . . .

We came out into a patio, crossed that and
went along a colonnaded arcade, emerged at
the edge of a stretch of blue-violet grass as
smooth as a billiard table, running down
across a wide slope to a line of trees with the
sheen of water beyond them. We followed a
tiled path beside flowering shrubs, rounded a
shallow pool where a fountain jetted liquid
sunshine into the air, arrived at a small
covered terrace, where a vast, elderly man
with a face like a clean-shaven Moses rested in
an elaborately padded chair.

"The Lord Pastaine," the servant said
casually and stepped to adjust the angle of the
old gentleman's chair to a more conversational position. Its occupant looked us over im-
passively, said, "Thank you, Dos," and indicated a pair of benches next to him. I introduced myself and Fsha-fsha and we sat. Dos
murmured an offer of refreshment and we
asked for a light wine. He went away and Lord
Pastaine gave me a keen glance.

"A Man from a very distant world," he said.
"A Man who is no stranger to violence." His
look turned to Fsha-fsha. "And a being equally
far from his home-world, tested also in the
crucible of adversity." He pushed his lips out

and looked thoughtful. "And what brings such adventurers here, to ancient Zeridajh, a world in the twilight of its greatness, to call upon an aged idler, dozing away the long afternoon of his life?"

"I met a lady, once, Milord," I said. "She was a long way from home—as far as I am, now, from mine. I tried to help her get home, but . . . things went wrong." I took a deep breath. "I'd like to know, sir, if the Lady Raire is here, safe, on Zeridajh."

His face changed, turned to wood. "The Lady Raire?" His voice had a thin, strained quality. "What do you know of her?"

"I was hired by Sir Orfeo," I said. "To help on the hunt. There was an accident. . . ." I gave him a brief account of the rest of the story. "I tried to find a lead to the H'eeaq," I finished. "But with no luck." It was on the tip of my tongue to tell him the rest, about Huvile and the glimpse I'd gotten of her, three years before, on Drath; but for some reason I didn't say it. The old man watched me all the while I talked. Then he shook his head.

"I am sorry, sir," he said, "that I have no good tidings for you."

"She never came back, then?"

His mouth worked. He started to speak, twice, then said, "No! The devoted child whom I knew was spirited away by stealth, by those whom I trusted, and never returned!"

I let that sink in. The golden light across the

wide lawn seemed to fade suddenly to a taw-
dry glare. The vision of the empty years rose
up in front of me.

". . . send out a search expedition," Fsha-
fsha was saying. "It might be possible—"

"The Lady Raire is dead!" the old man
raised his voice. "Dead! Let us speak of other
matters!"

The servant brought the wine, and I tried to
sip mine and make small talk, but it wasn't a
success. Across the lawn a servant in neat
gray livery was walking a leashed animal
along a path that sparkled blood-red in the
afternoon sun. The animal didn't seem to like
the idea of a stroll. He planted all four feet
and pulled backward. The man stopped and
mopped at his forehead while the reluctant
pet sat on his haunches and yawned. When he
did that, I was sure. I hadn't seen a cat for
almost three years, but I knew this one. His
name was Eureka.

CHAPTER ELEVEN

Ten minutes later, as Fsha-fsha and I crossed the lawn toward the house, a broad-shouldered man with curled gray hair and an elegantly simple tunic emerged from a side path ahead.

"You spoke to His Lordship of Milady Raire?" he said in a low voice as we came up.

"That's right."

He jerked his head toward the house. "Come along to where we can talk quietly. Perhaps we can exchange information to our mutual advantage." He led us by back passages into the deep, cool gloom of a room fitted up like an office for a planetary president. He told us his name was Sir Tanis, and got out a flagon and glasses and poured a round.

"The girl reappeared three months ago," he said. "Unfortunately," he added solemnly, "she is quite insane. Her first act was to disavow all her most hallowed obligations to the House of Ancinet-Chanore. Now, I gather from the few scraps of advice that reached my ears—"

"Dos talks as well as listens, I take it," I said.

"A useful man," Sir Tanis agreed crisply. "As I was saying, I deduce that you know something of Milady's activities while away from home. Perhaps you can tell me something which might explain the sad disaffection that afflicts her."

"Why did Lord Pastaine lie to us?" I countered.

"The old man is in his dotage," he snapped. "Perhaps, in his mind, she *is* dead." His lips quirked in a mirthless smile. "He's unused to rebellion among the very young." The brief smile dropped. "But she didn't stop with asserting her contempt for His Lordship's doddering counsels; she spurned as well the advice of her most devoted friends!"

"Advice on what?"

"Family matters," Tanis said shortly. "But you were about to tell me what's behind her incomprehensible behavior."

"Was I?"

"I assumed as much—I confided in you!" Tanis looked thwarted. "See here, if it's a matter of, ah, compensation for services rendered . . ."

"Maybe you'd better give me a little more background."

He looked at me sternly. "As you're doubtless aware, the House of Ancinet-Chanore is one of the most distinguished on the planet," he said. "We trace our lineage back through eleven thousand years, to Lord Ancinet of Travai. Naturally, such a house enjoys a deserved preeminence among its peers. And the head of that house must be an individual of the very highest attainments. Why . . ." he looked indignant, "if the seat passed to anyone but myself, in a generation—less! we should deteriorate to the status of a mere fossil, lacking in all finesse in the arts that mark a truly superior seat!"

"What's the Lady Raire got to do with all that?"

"Surely you're aware. Why else are you here?"

"Pretend we're not."

"The girl is an orphan," Sir Tanis said shortly. "Of the primary line. In addition . . ." he sounded exasperated, ". . . all the collateral heirs—all! are either dead, exiled, or otherwise disqualified in the voting!"

"So?"

"She—a mere girl, utterly lacking in experience—other than whatever bizarre influences she may have come under during her absence—holds in her hands five ballots! Five, out of nine! *She*—ineligible herself, of course, on a number of counts—controls the selection of the next head of this house! Why else do you imagine she was kidnapped?"

"Kidnapped?"

He nodded vigorously. "And since her return, she's not only rebuffed my most cordial offers of association—but has alienated every other conceivable candidate as well. In fact . . ." he lowered his voice, "it's my personal belief the girl intends to lend her support to an Outsider!"

"Sir Tanis, I guess all this family politics business is pretty interesting to you, but it's over my head like a wild pitch. I came here to see Milady Raire, to find out if she was safe and well. First I'm told she's dead, then that she's lost her mind. I'd like to see for myself. If you could arrange—"

"No," he said flatly. "That is quite impossible."

"May I ask why?"

"Sir Revenat would never allow it. He closets her as closely as a prize breeding soumi."

"And who's Sir Revenat?"

He raised his eyebrows. "Her husband," he said. "Who else?"

"Tough," Fsha-fsha consoled me as we

walked along the echoing corridor, following the servant Sir Tanis had assigned to lead us back into the outside world. "Not much joy there; but at least she's home, and alive."

We crossed an inner court where a fountain made soft music, and a door opened along the passage ahead. An elderly woman, thin, tight-corseted, dressed in a chiton of shimmering white, spoke to the servant, who faded away like smoke. She turned and looked at me with sharp eyes, studied Fsha-fsha's alien face.

"You've come to help her," she said to him in a dry, husky voice. "You know, and you've come to her aid."

"Ah . . . whose aid, Milady?" he asked her.

The old lady grimaced and said: "The Lady Raire's; she's in mortal danger; that's why her father ordered her sent away, on his death-bed! But none of them will believe me."

"What kind of danger is she in?"

"I don't know—but it's there, thick in the air around her! Poor child, so all alone."

"Milady," I stepped forward. "I've come a long way. I want to see her before I go. Can you arrange it?"

"Of course, you fool, else why would I have lain here in wait like a mud-roach over a wine-arbor?" She returned her attention to Fsha-fsha. "Tonight—at the Gathering of the House. Milady will be present; even Sir Revenat wouldn't dare defy custom so far as to deny her; and you shall be there, too! Listen! This is what you must do. . . ."

Half an hour later, we were walking along a tiled street of craftsmen's shops that was worn to a pastel smoothness that blended with the soft-toned facades that lined it. There were flowers in beds and rows and urns and boxes and in hanging trays that filtered the early light over open doorways where merchants fussed over displays of goods. I could smell fresh-baked bread and roasting coffee, and leather and wood-smoke. It was an atmosphere that made the events inside the ancient House of Ancinet-Chanore seem like an afternoon with the Red Queen.

"If you ask me, the whole bunch of them is round the bend," Fsha-fsha said. "I think the old lady had an idea I was in touch with the spirit world."

On a bench in front of a carpenter's stall, a man sat tapping with a mallet and chisel at a slab of tangerine-colored wood. He looked up and grinned at me.

"As pretty a bit of emberwood as ever a man laid steel to, eh?" he said.

"Strange," Fsha-fsha said. "You only see hand labor on backward worlds and rich ones. On all the others, a machine would be squeezing a gob of plastic into whatever shape was wanted."

In another stall, an aged woman was looming a rug on rich-colored fibers. Across the way, a boy sat in an open doorway, polishing what looked like a second-hand silver chalice. Up ahead, I saw the tailor shop the old woman —Milady Bezaille her name was—had told us about. An old fellow with a face like an elf was rolling out a bolt of green cloth with a texture like hand-rubbed metal. He looked up and ducked his head as we came in. "Ah, the sirs desire a change of costume?"

Fsha-fsha was already feeling the green stuff. "How about an outfit made of this?"

"Ah, the being has an eye," the old fellow cackled. "Radiant, is it not? Loomed by Y'sallo, of course."

I picked out a black like a slice of midnight in the Fringe. The tailor flipped up the end of the material and whirled it around my shoulders, stepped back and studied the effect thoughtfully.

"I see the composition as an expression of experience," he nodded. "Yes, it's possible. Stark, unadorned—but for the handsome necklace—Riv work is it not? Yes, a statement of self-affirmation, an incitement to discipline."

He went to work measuring and clucking. When he started cutting, we crossed a small bridge to a park where there were tables on

the lawn beside a small bridge to a park
where there were tables on the lawn beside a
small lemon-yellow dome. We sat and ate
pastries and then went along to a shoemaker,
who sliced into glossy hides and in an hour
had fitted new boots to both of us. When we
got back to the tailor shop, the new clothes
were waiting. We asked directions to a re-
fresher station, and, after an ion-bath and a
little attention to my hair and Fsha-fsha's gill
fringes, tried out our new costumes.

"You're an impressive figure," Fsha-fsha
said admiringly. "In spite of your decorations, your size and muscular develop-
ment give you a certain animal beauty; and I
must say the little tailor set you off to best
advantage."

"The high collar helps," I conceded. "But
I'm afraid the eye-patch spoils the effect."

"Wrong; it enhances the impression of an
elegant corsair."

"Well, if the old Tree could see you now, it
would have to admit you're the fanciest nut
that ever dropped off it," I said.

It was twilight in the parklike city. We still
had an hour to kill, and decided to use it in a
stroll around the Old Town—the ancient
marketplace that was the original center of
the city. It was a picturesque place, and we
were just in time to see the merchants folding
up their stalls, and streaming away to the
drinking terraces under the strung lights
among the trees. The sun set in a glory of

painted clouds; the brilliant spread of stars
that covered the sky like luminous clotted
cream was obscured by the overcast. The
empty streets dimmed into deep shadow, as
we turned our steps toward the gates of the
estate Ancinet-Chanore.

My sense-booster was set at 1.3 normal; any
higher setting made ordinary sound and light
levels painful. For the last hundred feet I had
been listening to the gluey wheeze that was
the sound of human lungs, coming from somewhere up ahead. I touched Fsha-fsha's arm.
"In the alley," I said softly. "Just one man."

He stepped ahead of me, and in the same instant a small, lean figure sprang into view
twenty feet ahead, stopped in a half-crouch
facing us, with his feet planted wide and his
gun hand up and aimed. I saw a lightning-
wink and heard the soft *whap!* of a filament
pistol. Fsha-fsha *oof!*ed as he took the bolt
square in the chest; a corona outlined his
figure in vivid blue as the harness bled the
energy off to the ground. Then he was on the
assassin; his arm rose and fell with the sound
of a hammer hitting a grapefruit, and the
would-be killer tumbled backward and slid
down the wall to sprawl on the pavement. I
went flat against the wall, flipped the booster

up to max, heard nothing but the normal night sounds of a city.

"Clear," I said. Fsha-fsha leaned over the little man.

"I hit him too hard," he said. "He's dead."

"Maybe the old lady was right," I said.

"Or maybe Sir Tanis wasn't as foolish as he sounded," Fsha-fsha grunted. "Or Milord Pastaine as senile as they claimed."

"A lot of maybes," I said. "Let's dump him out of sight and get out of here, in case a cleanup squad is following him up."

We lifted him and tossed him in the narrow passage he had picked as a hiding place.

"Which way?" Fsha-fsha asked.

"Straight ahead, to the main gates," I said.

"You're still going there—after this?"

"More than ever. Somebody made a mistake, sending a hit man out. They made a second not making it stick. We'll give them a chance to go for three."

The Lady Bezaille had given instructions to the gatekeeper; he bowed us through like visiting royalty into an atmosphere of lights and sounds and movement. The grand celebration known as the Gathering of the House seemed to be going on all over the grounds and throughout the house. We made our way through the throngs of beautiful people, looking for a familiar face. Sir Tanis popped up and gave a lifted-eyebrow look, but there wasn't enough surprise there to make him the man behind the assassination attempt.

"Captain Danger; Sir Fsha-fsha; I confess I didn't expect to see you here. . . ." He was aching to ask by whose order we were included in the select gathering, but apparently his instinct for the oblique approach kept him from asking.

"It seemed the least I could do," I said in what I hoped was a cryptic tone. "By the way, has Milady Raire arrived yet?"

"Ha! She and Lord Revenat will make a dramatic entrance after the rest of us have been allowed to consume ourselves in restless patience for a time, you can be sure."

He led us to the nearest refreshment server, which dispensed foamy concoctions in big tulip glasses; we stood on the lawn and fenced with him verbally for a few minutes, parted with an implied understanding that whatever happened, our weight would go to the side of justice—whatever that meant.

Milady Bezaille appeared, looked us over and gave a sniff that seemed to mean approval of our new finery. I had a feeling she'd regretted her earlier rash impulse of inviting two space tramps to the grand soiree of the year.

"Look sharp, now," she cautioned me. "When Milord Revenat deigns to appear he'll be swamped at once with the attentions of certain unwholesome elements of the House; that will be your chance to catch a glimpse of Milady Raire. See if you read in her face other than pain and terror!"

A slender, dandified lad sauntered over after the beldame had whisked away.

"I see the whole lady is attempting to influence you," he said. "Beware of her, sirs. She is not of sound mind."

"She was just tipping us off that the punch in number three bowl is spiked with hand-blaster pellets," I assured him. He gave me a quick, sideways look.

"What, ah, did she say to you about Sir Fane?"

"Ah-hah!" I nodded.

"Don't believe it!" he snapped. "Lies! Damnable lies!"

I edged closer to him. "What about Sir Tanis?" I muttered.

He shifted his eyes. "Watch him. All his talk about unilateral revisionism and ancillary line vigor—pure superstition."

"And Lord Revenat?"

He looked startled. "You don't mean—" he turned and scuttled away without finishing the sentence.

"Danger—are you sure this is the right place we're in?" Fsha-fsha whispered. "If the Lady Raire is anything like the rest of this menagerie. . . ."

"She isn't," I said. "She—"

I stopped talking as a stir ran through the little conversational groups around us. Across the lawn a servant in crimson livery was towing a floating floodlight along above the heads of a couple just descending a wide, shallow flight of steps from a landing terrace above. I hadn't seen the heli arrive. The man was tall, wide-shouldered, trim, like all Zeridajhans, dressed in a form-fitting wine-colored outfit with an elaborate pectoral ornament suspended around his neck on a chain. The woman beside him was slim, elegantly gowned in a silvery gauze, with her black hair piled high, intricately entwined in a jeweled coronet. I'd never seen her in jewels before but that perfect face, set in an expression that was the absence of all expression, was that of Milady Raire.

The crowd had moved in their direction as if by a common impulse to rush up and greet the newcomers; but the movement halted and the restless murmur of chatter resumed, but with a new, nervous note that was evident in the shrill cackle of laughter and the over-hearty waving of arms. I made my way across through the crowd, watching the circle of impressively clad males collecting around the newcomers. They moved off in a body, with a

great deal of exuberant joking that sounded
about as sincere as a losing politician's con-
gratulatory telegram to the winner

I trailed along at a distance of ten yards,
while the group swirled around a drink dis-
penser and broke up into a central group and
half a dozen squeezed-out satellites. The lucky
winners steered their prize on an evasion
course, dropping a few members along the
way when clumsy footwork involved them in
exchanges of amenities with other, less favor-
ed groups. In five minutes, the tall man in the
burgundy tights was fenced into a corner by
half a dozen hardy victors, while the lady in
silver stood for the moment alone at a few
yards distance.

I looked at her pale, aloof face, still as
youthful and unlined as it had been seven
years ago, when we last talked together under
the white sun of Gar 28. I took a deep breath
and started across the lawn toward her.

She didn't notice me until I was ten feet
from her; then she turned slowly and her eyes
went across me as coolly as the first breath of
winter. They came back again, and this time
flickered—and held on me. Suddenly I was
conscious of the scar, two-thirds concealed by
the high collar of my jacket, that marked the
corner of my jaw—and of the black patch over
my right eye. Her eyes moved over me, back
to my face. They widened; her lips parted,
then I was standing before her.

"Milady Raire," I said, and heard the hoarse note in my voice.

"Can . . . can it be . . . *you*?" Her voice was the faintest of whispers.

A hard hand took my arm, spun me around.

"I do not believe, sir," a furious voice snarled, "that you have the privilege of approach to Her Ladyship—" He got that far before his eyes took in what they were looking at; his voice trailed off. His mouth hung open. He dropped my arm and took a step back. It was the man named Huvile.

"Sir Revenat," someone started, and let it drop. I could almost hear his mind racing, looking for the right line to take. But nobody, even someone who had only talked to me for five minutes three years before, could pretend to have forgotten my face: black-skinned, scarred, one-eyed.

"It . . . it . . . I . . ."

"Sir Revenat," I said as smoothly as I could under the circumstances, and gave him a stiff little half-bow. That passed the ball to him. He could play it any way he liked from there.

"Why, why . . ." He took my arm, in a gentler grip this time. "My dear fellow! What an extraordinary pleasure. . . ." His eyes went to Milady Raire. She returned a look as impersonal as the carved face of a statue. She didn't look at me.

"If you will excuse us, Milady," Huvile/Revenat ducked his head and hustled me past her, and the silent crowd parted to let us through.

Inside a white damask room with a wall of glass through which the lights of the garden cast a soft polychrome glow, Huvile faced me. He looked a little different than he had the last time I had seen him, wearing the coarse kilt of a slave in the household of the Triarch of Drath. He had lost the gaunt look and was trimmed, manicured and polished like a prize-winning boar.

"You've . . . changed," he said. "For a moment, I almost failed to recognize you." His voice was hearty enough, but his eyes were as alert as a coiled rattler's.

I nodded. "A year on the Triarch's rafts have that effect."

"The rafts?" He looked shocked. "But . . . . but . . ."

"The penalty for freeing slaves," I said. "And not being able to pay the fines."

"But . . . I assumed . . ."

"Everything I owned was on my boat," I said.

His face was turning darker, as if pressure was building up behind it. "Your boat . . . I . . . ah . . ." he made an effort to get hold of himself. "See here, didn't you direct, ah, the young woman to lift ship at once?" His look told me he was waiting to see if I'd pick up the impersonal reference to the Lady Raire. I shook my head and waited.

"But—she arrived a moment or two after I reached the port. You *did* send her?"

"Yes—"

"Of course," he hurried on. "She seemed most distraught, poor creature. I explained to her that a kindly stranger—yourself—had purchased my freedom—and presumably hers as well—and while we spoke, a creature appeared; a ghastly-looking little beggar. The unfortunate girl was terrified by the sight of him; I drove the thing off, and then . . . and then she insisted that we lift at once!" Huvile shook his head, looking grieved. "I understand now; in her frenzy to make good her escape, she abandoned you, her unknown savior. . . ." A thought hit him, sharpened his eyes. "You hadn't, ah, personally known the poor child?"

"I saw her for a moment at the Triarch's palace—from a distance."

He sighed. His look got more comfortable. "A tragedy that your kindness was rewarded by such ingratitude. Believe me, sir, I am eternally in your debt! I acknowledge it freely. . . ." He lowered his voice. "But let us keep the details in confidence, between us. It would not be desirable at this moment, to introduce a new factor, however extraneous, into the somewhat complex equations of House affairs." He was getting expansive now. "We shouldn't like my ability to reward you as you deserve suffer through any fallacious construction that might be put on matters, eh?"

"I take it you took the female slave under your wing," I said.

He gave me a sharp look. He would have liked her left out of the conversation.

"She would have needed help to get home," I amplified.

"Ah, yes, I think I see now," he smiled a sad, sweet smile. "You were taken with her beauty. But alas . . ." his eyes held on mine, "she died."

"That's very sad," I said. "How did it happen?"

"My friend, wouldn't it be better to forget her? Who knows what terrible pressures might not have influenced her to the despicable course she chose? Poor waif; she suffered greatly. Her death gave her surcease." His expression became brisk. "And now, in what way can I serve you, sir? Tell me how I can make amends for the injustice done you."

He talked some more, offered me the hospitality of the estate, a meal, even, delicately, money. His relief when I turned them down was obvious. Now that he saw I wasn't going to be nasty about the little misunderstanding, his confidence was coming back. I let him ramble on. When he ran down, I said:

"How about an introduction to the lady in silver? The Lady Raire, I understand her name is."

His face went hard. "That is impossible. The lady is not well. Strange faces upset her."

"Too bad," I said. "In that case, I guess there's not much for me to stay around for."

"Must you go? But of course if you have business matters requiring your attention, I mustn't keep you." He went across to an archway leading toward the front of the house; he was so eager to get rid of me the easy way that he almost fell down getting there. He didn't realize I'd turned the opposite way and stepped back out onto the terrace, until I was already across it and heading across the lawn to where Milady Raire still stood alone, like a pale statue in the winking light of an illuminated fountain.

She watched me come across the lawn to her. I could hear the hurrying footsteps of Sir

Revenat behind me, not quite running, heard
someone intercept him, the babble of self-
important voices. I walked up to her and my
eyes held on her face; it was as rigid as a death
mask.

"Milady, what happened after you left
Drath?" I asked her without preamble.

"I—" she started and her eyes showed
shock. "Then—on Drath—it was you—"

"You're scared, Milady. They're all scared
of Huvile, but you most of all. Tell me why."

"Billy Danger," she said, and for an instant
the iron discipline of her face broke, but she
caught herself. "Fly, Billy Danger," she whispered in English. "Fly hence in the instant, ere
thou, too, art lost, for nothing can rescue me!"

I heard feet coming up fast behind me and
turned to see Sir Revenat, his face white with
fury, masked by a ghastly grin.

"You are elusive, my friend," he grated. His
fingers were playing with the heavy ornament
dangling on his chest, an ovoid with a half-
familiar look. . . . "I fear you've lost your way.
The gate lies at the opposite end of the gardens." His hand reached for me as if to guide
me back to the path, but I leaned aside from
it, turned to Milady Raire. I put out my hand
as if to offer it to her, instead reached farther,
ran my fingers down her silken side—and felt
the slight, telltale lump there. She gasped and
drew back. Huvile let out a roar and caught at
my arm savagely. A concerted gasp had gone

up from every mouth within gasping range.

"Barbarian wretch!" Huvile howled. "You'd lay hands on the person of a lady of the House of Ancinet Chanore . . ." the rest was just an inarticulate bellow backed up by a chorus of the same from the assembled spectators.

"Enough!" Huvile yelled. "This adventurer comes among us to mock the dignity and honor of this house, openly offers insult to a noble lady of the ancient line!" He whirled to face the crowd. "Then I'll oblige him with a taste of that just fury of that line! Milords! Bring me my sword box!" He turned back to me, and there was red fury enough in his eyes for ten houses. He stepped close, put his face close to mine. His fingers played with the slave controller at his neck. I judged the distance for a jump, but he was ready with his finger on the control. And we both knew that a touch by anyone but himself would activate it.

"You saw," he hissed. "You know her life is in my hands. If you expose me, she dies!"

CHAPTER TWELVE

The lords and ladies of the House of Ancinet-Chanore may have been out of touch with reality in some ways, but when it came to setting up the stage for a blood-duel on their fancy lawn under the gay lights, they were the soul of efficiency. While a ring of armed servants stood obtrusively around me, others hurried away and came back with a fancy inlaid box of darkly polished wood. Huvile lifted the lid with a flourish and took out a straight-bladed saber heavy enough to behead a peasant with. There was a lot of gold thread and jewel-work around the hilt, but it was a butcher's weapon. Another one, just like it but without the jelly beans was trotted out for me.

Sir Tanis made the formal speech; he cited all the hallowed customs that surrounded the

curious custom that allowed an irate Lord of
the House to take a cleaver to anyone who an-
noyed him sufficiently, and then in a less pom-
pous tone explained the rules to me. They
weren't much: we'd hack at each other until
Sir Revenat was satisfied or dead.

"Man to man," Sir Tanis finished his spiel.
"The House of Ancinet-Chanore defends its
honor with the ancient right of its strong arm!
Let her detractors beware!"

Then the crowd backed off and the servants
formed up a loose ring, fifty feet across.
Huvile brandished his sword and his eyes ate
me alive. Fsha-fsha took my jacket and leaned
close to me a last word of advice.

"Remember your Sorting training, Billy
Danger! Key-in your response patterns to his
attack modes! Play him until you read him
like a glorm-bulb line! Then strike!"

"If I don't make it," I said, "find a way to
tell them."

"You'll make it," he said. "But—yeah—I'll
do my best."

He withdrew at a curt command from Tanis, and Huvile moved out to meet me. He held
the sword lightly, as if his wrist was used to
handling it. I had an idea the upstart sir had
spent a lot of hours practicing the elevating
art of throwing his weight around. He moved
in with the blade held low, pointed straight at
me. I imitated his stance. He made a small
feint and I slapped his blade with mine and
moved back as he dropped his point and lung-

ed and missed my thigh by an inch. I tried to blank my mind, key in his approach-feint-attack gambit to a side-jump-and-counter-cut syndrome. It was hard to bring the pattern I wanted into clear focus without running through it, physically. I backed, made Huvile blink by doing the jump and cut in pantomime, two sword-lengths from contact distance. A nervous titter ran through the audience, but that was all right. I was pretty sure I'd set the response pattern I wanted to at least one of his approaches. But he had others.

He came after me, cautious now, checking me out. He tried a high thrust, a low cut, a one-two lunge past my guard. I backed shamelessly, for each attack tried to key-in an appropriate response—

I felt myself whip to one side, slash in an automatic reaction to a repetition of his opening gambit. My point caught his sleeve and ripped through the wine-red cloth. So far so good. Huvile back-pedaled, then tried a furious frontal attack; I gave ground, my arm countering him with no conscious thought on my part. He realized the tactic was getting him nowhere and dropped his point, whipped it up suddenly as he dived forward. I caught it barely in time, deflected the blade over my right shoulder, and was chest to chest with him, our hilts locked together.

"It's necessary for me to kill you," he whispered. "You understand that it's impossible for me to let you live." His eyes looked mad; his free hand still gripped the controller. "If I die—she dies. And if I suspect you may be gaining—I plunge the lever home. Your only choice is to sacrifice yourself." He pushed me away and jabbed a vicious cut at me and then we were circling again. My brain seemed to be set in concrete. Huvile was nuts—no doubt about that. He had brazened his way into the midst of the House of Ancinet-Chanore on the strength of the invisible knife he held at Milady's heart; and if he saw the game was up—the fragile game he'd nursed along for months now—he'd kill her with utter finality and in the most incredible agony, as the magnesium flare set in her heart burned its way through her ribs.

There was just one possibility. The Drathians had gone to a lot of trouble to link the life of the slave to the well-being of the master; but there was one inevitable weak spot. Even the most sophisticated circuitry couldn't do its job after it was destroyed. I'd proven that; I had crushed Huvile's controller under my foot—and he was still alive.

But on the other hand, maybe that had been a freak, a defective controller. Huvile had been two miles away at the time. And it was no special trick to rig an electronic device so that the cut-off of a carrier signal actuated a response in a receiver....

There was sweat on my face, not all of it from the exercise. My only chance was to smash the controller and kill Huvile with the same stroke—and hope for the best. Because, win or lose, the Lady Raire was better dead than slave to his madman.

While these merry thoughts were racing through my mind, I was backing, feinting and parrying automatically. And suddenly Huvile's blade dropped, flickered in at me and out again and I felt my right leg sag and go out from under me. I caught myself in time to counter an over-eager swing and strike back from one knee, but it was only a moment's delay of the inevitable. I saw his arm swing back for the finishing stroke—

There was swirl of silver, and the Lady Raire was at his side, clutching his sword arm—and then she crumpled, white-faced, as the controller's automatic angina circuit clamped iron fingers on her heart. But it was enough. While Huvile staggered, off-balance, his free hand groping, I came up in a one-legged lunge. He saw me, brought his sword up and back, at the same time snatched for the controller. He was a fraction of a second late. My point struck it, burst it into chips, slammed on through bone and muscle and lodged in his spine. He fell slowly, with an amazed look on his face. I saw him hit; then I went over sideways and grabbed for the gaping wound in my thigh and felt darkness close in.

The House of Ancinet-Chanore was very manly about acknowledging its mistake. I sat across from old Lord Pastaine under the canopy on his favorite sun terrace, telling him for the sixth or seventh time how it had happened that I had bought freedom for two slaves and then sent them off together in my boat while I went to the rafts. He wagged his Mosaic head and looked grave.

"A serious misjudgment of character on your part," he said. "Yet were we not all guilty of misjudgment? When the Lady Raire returned, so unexpectedly, I wished to open my heart to her—suppose—savior. I granted the interloper—Huvile, you say his name was?" He shook his head. "An upstart, of no family—I granted him, I say, every freedom, every honor in the gift of Ancinet-Chanore. As for Milady—if she chose to closet herself in solitary withdrawal from the comfort of her family—could I say nay? And then I saw the beginnings of the wretched maneuverings that would make this stranger Head after my death. I called for Milady Raire to attend me—and she refused! Me! It was unheard of! Can you blame me for striking her from my memory, as one dead? And as for the others— venal, grasping, foolish—to what depths has the House not fallen since the days of my youth, a thousand years agone. . . ."

I listened to him ramble on. I had been hearing the same story from a variety of directions during the past three days, while my leg healed under the miracle-medicines of old Zeridajh. If any one of the Lady Raire's doting relations had cared enough about her to take just one, good, searching look into her eyes, they'd have seen that something was seriously amiss. But all they saw was a pawn on the board of House politics, and her silent appeals had gone unanswered. As for why she hadn't defied Huvile, faced death before submitting to enslavement to his ambitions—I could guess that half an hour of sub-fatal angina might be a persuasion that would convince a victim who could laugh at the threat of mere death.

"If you'd arrange for me to see the Lady Raire for a few minutes," I butted in Milord's rumbling assessment of the former Sir Revenat's character, "I'd be most appreciative."

He looked grave. "I believe we all agree that it would be best not to reawaken the unhappy emotions of these past months by any references thereto," he said. "We are grateful to you, Captain Danger—the House will be forever in your debt. I'm sure Milady will understand if you slip quietly away, leaving her to the ministrations of her family, those who know where her interests lie."

I got the idea. It had been explained to me in slightly varying terms by no less than twelve solemn pillars of the House of Ancinet-Chanore. The Lady Raire, having had one close brush with an interloper, would not be exposed to the questionable influences of another. They were glad I'd happened along in time to break the spell—but now the lady would return to her own kind, her own life.

And they were right, of course. I didn't know just what it was that Jongo would have to say to Milady Raire of the ancient House of Ancinet-Chanore; I'd had my share of wild fancies, but none of them were wild enough to include offering her boudoir space aboard my boat as an alternative to the estate of Ancinet-Chanore.

On the way out, Sir Tanis offered me a crack at a lot of fancy trade opportunities, letters of recommendation to any house I might name, and assorted other vague rewards, and ended with a hint, none too closely veiled, that any further attempt to see the lady would end unhappily for me. I told him I got the idea and walked out into the twilight through the high gates of the house with no more than a slight limp to remind me of my visit.

Fsha-fsha was waiting for me at the boat. I told him about my parting interviews with the House of Ancinet-Chanore. He listened.

"You never learn, do you, Billy?" he wagged his head sadly.

"I've learned that there's no place for me in fancy company," I said. "Give me the honest solitude of space, and a trail of new worlds waiting ahead. That's my style."

"You saved the lady's life on Gar 28, you know," Fsha-fsha said, talking to himself. "If you hadn't done what you did—when you did —she'd never have lived out the first week. It was too bad you didn't look and listen a bit before you handed her over to the H'eeaq—but then, who would have known, eh?"

"Let's forget all that," I suggested. "The ship's trimmed to lift—"

"Then at Drath, you picked her out from under the Triarch's nose in as smooth a counter-swindle as I've ever heard of. He had no idea of letting them go, you know. They'd have been arrested at the port—except that the Rule-keepers were caught short when the tub lifted without you. Your only mistake was in trusting Huvile—"

"Trusting Huvile!"

"You trusted him. You sent him along to an unguarded ship. If you'd worked just one angle a little more subtly—gone out yourself to see the lady aboard and then lifted, leaving Huvile behind—but this is neither here nor there. For the second time, you saved her—and handed her over to her enemy."

"I know that," I snapped. "I've kicked myself for it—"

"And now—here you are, repeating the pattern," he bored on. "Three times and out."

"What?"

"You saved the lady again, Billy. Plucked her out of the wicked hands of her tormentor—"

"And . . . ?"

"And handed her over to her enemies."

"Her family has her—"

"That's what I said."

"Then. . . ." Wheels were beginning to whirl in front of my eyes.

"Maybe," I said, "you'd better tell me exactly what you're talking about. . . ."

. . . She opened her eyes, startled, when I leaned over her sleeping couch.

"Billy Danger," she breathed. "Is it thee? Why came you not to me ere now?"

"An acute attack of stupidity, Milady," I whispered.

She smiled a dazzling smile. "My name is Raire, Billy. I am no one's lady."

"You're mine," I said.

"Always, my Billy." She reached and drew my face down to hers. Her lips were softer even than I had dreamed.

"Come," I said.

She rose silently and Eureka rubbed himself across her knees. They followed me across the wide room, along a still corridor. In the great hall below, I asked her to show me the shortest route to the grounds. She led the way along a cloistered arcade, through a walled garden, onto a wide terrace above the dark sweep of sky-lit lawn.

"Billy—when I pass this door, the house alarms will be set off. . . ."

"I know. That's why I dropped in on the roof in a one-man heli. Too bad we couldn't leave the same way. There's no help for it. Let's go. . . ."

We started out at a run toward the trees. We had gone fifty feet when lights sprang up across the back of the house. I turned and took aim with my filament gun and knocked out the two biggest polyarcs, and we sprinted for cover, Eureka loping in the lead. A new light sprang up, just too late, swept the stretch of grass we had just crossed. We reached the trees, went flat. Men were coming through the rear doors of the house. There was a lot of yelling. I looked up. Against the swirls and clots of stars, nothing was visible. I checked my watch again; Fsha-fsha was two minutes late. The line of men was moving down across the lawn. In half a minute, they'd reach the trees.

There was a wink of light from above, followed by a dull *baroom!* as of distant thunder. A high, whistling screech became audible, descended to a full-throated roar; something flashed overhead—a long shape ablaze with lights. A second gunboat slammed across in the wake of the first.

"That cuts it," I said. "Fsha-fsha's been picked off—"

A terrific detonation boomed, drawling itself out into a bellow of power. I saw a dark shape flash past against the clotted stars. The men on the lawn saw it, too. They halted their advance, looking up at the dark boat that had shot past on an opposite course to the security cutters.

"Look!" The Lady Raire pointed. Something big and dark was drifting toward our position across the lake. It was *Jongo III*, barely a yard above the surface of the water, concealed from the house by the trees. We jumped up and ran for it. Her bow lights came on, dazzling as suns, traversed over us, lanced out to blind the men beyond the trees. I could see the soft glow from her open entry-port. We splashed out into knee-deep water; I tossed Eureka in, then jumped, caught the rail, pulled myself in, reached back for the Lady Raire as men burst through the screen of trees. Then we were inside, pressed flat against the floor by the surge of acceleration as the old racer lifted and screamed away at treetop level at a velocity that would have boiled the surface off any lesser hull.

From a distance of half a million miles, Zeridajh was a misty emerald crescent, dwindling on our screens.

"It was a pretty world, Milady," I said. "You're going to miss it."

"Dost know what place I truly dreamed of, my Billy, when the gray years of Drath lengthened before me?"

"The gardens," I suggested. "They're very beautiful, with the sun on them."

"I dreamt of the caves, and the green shade of the giant peas, and the simple loyalty of our good Eureka...." She stroked the grizzled head resting on her knee.

"Never," Fsha-fsha said from the depths of the big command chair, "will I understand the motivations of you Propagators. Still, life in your company promises to be diverting, I'll say that for it." He showed us that ghastly expression he used for a smile. "But tell me, Milady—if the question isn't impertinent: what were you doing out there, at the far end of the Eastern Arm, where Billy first saw you?"

"Haven't you guessed?" she smiled at him. "Until Lord Desroy caught me, I was running away."

"I knew it!" Fsha-fsha boomed. "And now that the great quest is finished—where to?"

"Anywhere," I said. I put my arm around Raire's flower-slim waist and drew her to me. "Anywhere at all."

The sweet hum of the mighty and ancient engines drummed softly through the deck. Together, we watched the blaze of Center move to fill the screens.

KEITH LAUMER

Buy them at your local bookstore or use this handy coupon:
Clip and mail this page with your order

TOR BOOKS—Reader Service Dept.
49 W. 24 Street, 9th Floor, New York, NY 10010

Please send me the book(s) I have checked above. I am enclosing
$_____ (please add $1.00 to cover postage and handling).
Send check or money order only—no cash or C.O.D.'s.

Mr./Mrs./Miss _____

Address _____

City _____ State/Zip _____

Please allow six weeks for delivery. Prices subject to change without
notice.

HARRY HARRISON

PHILIP JOSÉ FARMER

☐	48534-4	THE CACHE	$2.75
☐	48504-2	FATHER TO THE STARS	$2.75
☐	48535-2	GREATHEART SILVER	$2.75
☐	40184-1	JESUS ON MARS	$1.95
☐	48508-5	OTHER LOG OF PHILEAS FOG	$2.50
☐	48529-8	THE PURPLE BOOK	$2.95
☐	48522-0	STATIONS OF THE NIGHTMARE	$2.75
☐	53766-1	TRAITOR TO THE LIVING	$2.95
☐	53767-X	Canada	$3.50

Buy them at your local bookstore or use this handy coupon:
Clip and mail this page with your order

TOR BOOKS—Reader Service Dept.
49 W. 24 Street, 9th Floor, New York, NY 10010

Please send me the book(s) I have checked above. I am enclosing
$_____ (please add $1.00 to cover postage and handling).
Send check or money order only—no cash or C.O.D.'s.

Mr./Mrs./Miss _____

Address _____

City _____ State/Zip _____

Please allow six weeks for delivery. Prices subject to change without
notice.

DAVID DRAKE